Love at Bay

A Gates Point Novel

Lynn Story

Published by Lynn Story, 2021.

LOVE AT BAY

First edition. July 5, 2021.

Copyright © 2021 Lynn Story.

ISBN: 978-1736787922

Written by Lynn Story.

Also by Lynn Story

A Gates Point Novel
Rescue My Love
Ginny's Christmas Wish
Love at Bay
The Primrose Heart
Love at Bay

Watch for more at www.stitchesandstories.com.

To Larry, with all my love.

"Ah, merciless Love, is there any length to which you cannot force the human heart to go?"
— **Virgil, The Aeneid**[1]

1.   https://www.goodreads.com/work/quotes/288738

CHAPTER ONE

"Portia asked me to go shopping and to lunch with her tomorrow after church, is that alright?"

"Portia?" I didn't think you liked her.

Blake paused while folding the laundry, perplexed by Jerry's comment, "Why would you think that? I've known her for years."

"Just because you've known someone for years doesn't mean you have to like her."

"Well, I do like Portia."

"What kind of shopping?"

"Oh, probably clothes and shoes."

"Don't you have enough shoes?" Jerry looked up from his laptop.

"Yes, I didn't say I was going to buy shoes, we are just having a girl's day to window shop and grab lunch."

"Just try to keep the spending to a minimum."

When Jerry wasn't looking, Blake rolled her eyes. He was constantly cautioning her about money. When had he become so worried about expenses? She and Jerry had never been frivolous; they put money aside each month and paid their bills on time; always careful not to live beyond their means; she worked at a large architectural firm making a decent salary; she didn't make as much as him, but she made darn close.

"Do you have plans tomorrow?" She asked, hoping he was going golfing or something so that he wouldn't text her asking when she was coming back home.

He puffed his chest out like he was trying to impress her, "Oh, me and the boys are playing over at the Crestwood."

"Crestwood? That is an expensive course." She mused aloud, irritated that he would ask her to watch her spending while he spent the day with his friends at one of the most exclusive golf clubs in the valley.

"Well, Ben is a member and so he gets a discount for bringing guests, but I'll probably have to buy lunch or a round of drinks."

"That sounds expensive."

Jerry snapped his laptop shut. Blake flinched at the sudden movement. He was very good at giving criticism and terrible at tolerating anything that hinted at a judgement of his own actions.

"I'm going out for a while." He grabbed his keys off the hook by the door.

Tempted to get in one more dig, Blake nearly asked when he would be back. But she was too grateful for the alone time, no matter how long it lasted. She smiled as the door slammed behind him. He was angry and on edge these days. Blake had learned long ago not to ask about work. She understood his firm handled large accounts, but it wasn't like his work was top secret.

"Finally." She said to the ceiling. Saturday's were the worst; Jerry worked all the time and treated Saturday like just another day at the office. Any music or sound from the TV caused him to rail about how he was trying to work to provide for them. Sunday's he usually did something with his friends and that gave her one day a week to watch whatever she wanted on TV or just sit and read a book. All of her friends took his attention as doting and told her how lucky she was. She felt like she was being ungrateful when she complained about his constant text messages. If she was out of the house for more than an hour on the weekends Jerry would start texting, asking when she would be home or what they were going to have for dinner. When she mentioned to Portia that she felt as if Jerry didn't trust her. Portia had told her she was lucky to have a man who cared about her so much. Blake wondered if she was the problem and not Jerry. Once she asked Pastor Sims about it, but he just patted her on the arm and said she was just going through a rough patch and she should pray about it with Jerry. She didn't believe praying was going to solve anything. Jerry played the part on Sunday mornings, but that was it. Praying was not his thing. She decided it was just her and she needed to work on improving her attitude.

***

Sunday afternoon hadn't arrived soon enough. She had practically run from the church, eager to get time away from the house.

"I'm leaving to play golf, what time are you meeting Portia?" Jerry announced as she was putting on her earrings upstairs in the bedroom.

"I'll be leaving in just a few minutes."

"Did you take anything out for dinner?"

"I'll do that before I leave. What would you like to have? If we are both having lunch out, I can make something light."

"I don't know we'll see."

She sighed. "Okay, I'll get something started."

"Whatever," He called from the stairs, already jangling his car keys.

There was just no winning with him. When had he become this demanding person? He had been so caring when they first married, now that caring was controlling. Or so she thought.

She ran downstairs to put a roast in the crock-pot. She needed to hurry so she wouldn't be late meeting Portia.

They spent a beautiful July afternoon window shopping in the open-air mall. They had lunch at the Magnolia Tea Room, and she had indulged in chocolate icebox pie. She was having such a wonderful time that she didn't notice until she was back in her car that Jerry hadn't texted her once. She smiled perhaps this was a turning point. She felt light and happy as she drove home listening to her favorite country music. When she pulled in the driveway, Jerry's car was already there. She thought it was odd that he parked outside. He always put his precious MG convertible in the garage, leaving her to scrape snow and ice off her car in the winter. She sensed something was wrong.

As she entered the house through the kitchen's side door, she called out, "Jerry, where are you?" She walked into the den and found him sitting on the sofa, drinking heavily. "What's wrong?"

"That bastard, Bernstein came to the club today," Jerry knocked back a shot, "to Crestwood and fired me! In front of everyone!"

Blake gasped, "What do you mean he fired you? How can he fire you?"

"Fired, means fired! So, I hope you had a good time today because it will be the last shopping spree you'll have for a while!" Jerry reached for the bottle of vodka sitting on the coffee table.

"Jerry, I'm so sorry, but we'll be okay. You'll find another job."

"You're going to have to pay the bills now." He sneered.

"I make almost as much as you. The bills won't be a problem. By the way, I bought nothing today and Portia paid for lunch."

"Good damn thing!" He stood up, wobbly.

"Are you hungry? I'll go check on dinner, food might help." She was looking for an escape. She had never seen him like this. It frightened her.

"No, I'm not hungry!" He pushed her out of the way and when he did, she fell back into the bookcase, knocking over a trophy he had won in a golf tournament. "Look what you've done, you stupid cow!"

"You pushed me!" Blake cried holding her head.

"You're lucky I don't do more than that!"

Blake stood up to face him, "Don't you dare touch me!" she screamed.

Jerry slapped her across the face. She hadn't expected the force of the blow, and her head snapped to the side and hit the bookshelf again.

Jerry stormed out of the room. With trembling hands and her head bleeding, Blake found her cell phone and called the police. No, it wasn't her fault. She wasn't the one who was selfish, and she saw that clearly now.

"911, what's your emergency?"

"My husband is drunk, and he hit me. I need the police."

"Are you okay, ma'am?"

"No! I'm not okay. I'm bleeding."

"Where is your husband now? Is he there with you?"

"He is in the house somewhere."

"Can you leave? Can you go to a neighbor's house where it is safe?"

"Yes, I can do that."

"Stay on the line with me."

"Okay."

Blake found she was a little unsteady on her own feet, but she made it out the front door just as Portia was pulling up in front of the house.

"Oh my god, Blake! What happened?"

"Jerry hit me!"

"What? Come on!" Portia led Blake to her car. "Have you called the police?"

Blake held up her phone. Portia reached over and took it.

"Hello?"

"911 dispatch, is someone there?"

"My name is Portia Carter, and I'm here with my friend, her husband has beat her, hurry, please!"

"Is your friend injured?"

"Yes, she has a head injury, I think she is going to pass out!"

Blake could hear the sirens in the distance as she leaned back in the passenger seat of Portia's car and closed her eyes.

"Ms. Townsend? Blake, can you hear me?"

Blake opened her eyes to see a woman leaning over her.

"Blake, we need to check your head wound, okay?"

"Okay" Blake said weakly.

"What is going on? Blake, what did you do?" Jerry shouted from across the lawn.

Portia stood at the front of her car while the paramedics examined Blake.

"What she do? You bastard!" Portia yelled back at him. "You actually hit her?"

Jerry looked stunned.

"Sir, please watch your head." The police officer guided Jerry into the backseat of the patrol car.

"Is she going to be alright?" Portia asked as the paramedics transferred Blake from her car to the gurney.

"We are going to take her to the hospital and have her examined further, but she likely has a mild concussion."

"Okay, I will follow you there. Blake, I'm going to go inside and get you a change of clothes and then I will meet you at the hospital, okay?"

Blake just nodded, too stunned by everything that was going on around her to speak. Her life seemed to have completely collapsed in one afternoon.

Portia took out her cell phone and called two more of Blake's friends and relayed what had happened. She asked them to meet her at the hospital.

An hour later, Blake was in the hospital surrounded by Portia, Meg and Amy.

"How are you?" Portia asked.

"Stunned."

"Oh honey, I feel just terrible about this," Meg took her hand.

"We all do," Portia agreed, "I should have listened to you when you said Jerry was being controlling. If we had listened, this wouldn't have happened." Portia looked like she was about to burst into tears.

"It's not your fault, or mine. It is his fault!" Blake said with conviction.

"Well, when we're done with him, that bastard won't know what hit him!" Meg reassured her.

"Excuse me," All eyes turned to the police officer standing in the doorway. "Ms. Townsend, I need to ask you a few questions."

"Okay."

"We'll be right outside if you need us." Portia reassured Blake and ushered the ladies into the hallway to wait.

"I want my husband out of my house, I don't want to have to see him ever again!" Blake demanded.

"Yes, ma'am we can file a restraining order have you consulted an attorney yet?"

"Not yet, but I will, my friend out there," She points towards the door, "her husband is an attorney and I'm sure she is calling him right now." She could see Portia on the phone.

"Okay, is there someplace you can stay for a while? A friend's house or a hotel?"

Blake nodded.

"Has your husband gotten physical before?"

"No, this is the first time, and the last time. He has always been controlling, but he has never hit me before today."

"What about today was different?"

"He got fired from his job."

"Where does your husband work?"

"Billington Financial Services."

"Okay, thank you. Try to get some rest." The officer smiled and left her business card.

Portia returned waving her phone, "Ted is on his way."

"We're going to take Jerry for everything he's got." Meg announced, looking from Portia to Amy.

"He doesn't have much, he got fired today. That's what set him off."

Portia sat down on the edge of the bed. "Really? Why?"

"He didn't say. Apparently, his boss fired him at the country club. It must have been pretty serious for him not to wait until Monday."

Portia's mind began racing. "I'll find out what's going on. Get some rest sweetie and tomorrow you are coming home with me. I've got to run but call me if you need anything."

"Thanks, Portia you're the best. Hey, why did you come by the house, anyway?"

"Oh, you left your scarf at the restaurant, I thought you might want it."

"Thanks."

"See ya soon."

Finally, alone Blake thought about what happened and cried quietly for losing herself and for the man Jerry used to be. She was angry; and didn't care about Jerry's money; she felt the need for revenge. If she could, she'd get out of the hospital bed and give him a taste of his own medicine. Obviously, that wasn't legal, or even possible at the moment. It also meant she would stoop to Jerry's level. She would wait for Ted, Portia's husband.

CHAPTER TWO

Six Months Later

"I wish you weren't leaving." Portia reached out to hug Blake one last time.

"I have to." Blake smiled sweetly. She would miss her friend and her hometown. It was time to break free to live her own life. It's a new year and a new me.

Portia nodded, fighting back a tear, "You call me the minute you get there and let me know you are safe."

"I will." Blake climbed into her Subaru Outback; a rental trailer hitched to the rear with a few things she couldn't live without from her old life. It had taken six months since she filed for divorce to get everything completed. Honestly, as ugly as things got with Jerry during the break-up, she was surprised that it had only taken six months. Jerry had gone from hating her to pleading with her not to go through with the divorce. He tried counseling, trying to get help. She only hoped that some of it took for the sake of the next woman in his life. But she was through with it all. She pulled away from the curb, waving goodbye to Portia.

She followed her GPS program. She had seen an article about the city of Gates Point in a gardening magazine; it seemed like such a picturesque place with a vibrant culture. She lived her entire life in Roanoke, but the thought of living along the water was inviting and exotic. Without a job lined up, she would have to rely on her savings and alimony. She was in no rush. She stopped once for a bite to eat and sat outside in the cool winter air, enjoying a cheeseburger while leaning against her car rereading the magazine that had set her on your journey to southeast Virginia. As she drove east, she was sure everything would be alright; she believed she had done what was best for her. Four hours later, she crossed the city line into Gates Point. Night was falling; the skyline was beautiful. She had booked ahead for a hotel until she got her bearings.

"Good Evening, may I help you?"

"Yes, reservation for Towns..." she almost used her married name, during the divorce she had returned to her maiden name, "Morgan, I have a reservation under Blake Morgan."

"Yes, I have it right here, welcome. Is this your first time visiting us?" The clerk asked.

"Yes, I am moving to Gates Point."

"Oh, you'll love it here. Our concierge has gone for the evening but if you stop by in the morning, she can help you get acquainted with the city and refer you to real estate services."

"Thank you, I appreciate that."

Blake collected her keycard and went in search of her room. She opened up the curtains to look out over her new home. The hotel was in the heart of the city. The skyline was amazing with tall buildings to the north and east of her. To the west it looked darker, fewer lights and she guessed the James River was in that direction. After settling in, she called Portia to let her know she arrived safely. She laid across the bed and contemplated her new life. It was exciting and scary, but she was free to make it whatever she wanted it to be. One thing she had decided on the drive out, she would not listen to country music anymore. Every song on the radio reminded her of her old life. She would reinvent herself, and for now she would start with her choice of music. She pulled out her copy of the magazine with the article about Gates Point; it listed some areas of interest such as the historic Garden District, the arts and crafts district, and a few others. It also listed notable musicians from the area, so she thought there must be a lot of wonderful music for her to experience. She would remember to ask the concierge about them tomorrow. Tonight, she thought about what kind of job she wanted. She wasn't sure if she wanted to return to her former profession as an architect; she hoped Jerry wouldn't try to find her, but if he did, he would start with the architectural firms. She thought she might try something different for a while.

With recommendations from the concierge, it didn't take long to find an apartment on the edge of the arts district. She had explored the Garden District, which had been featured in the magazine article, but it was out of her price range even some carriage houses cost more than her new apartment. She found a local college with an Architectural program and applied for a lecturer position. Even if she got an interview and the job it was already mid-January so the soonest, she could start teaching would be May. In the meantime, she set about exploring Gates Point. There was a locally owned grocery store close to her apartment, its part grocery store, part indoor farmer's market. The seafood was so fresh that they kept it in larger coolers packed in ice on the floor. They didn't quite have everything, and she was sure if she drove a little further away, she would find a chain grocery store. But she liked the idea of walking to the market and supporting a local business. To her delight, she discovered an independent bookstore along her route and popped in to see what they offered. The sign pained on the large windows read 'Bumboat Books New and Used'. She breathed in the smell of books as she walked through the door. It was a comforting scent. It reminded her of a bookstore back home that she used to visit with her mother ever Saturday when she was little. The books allowed her to escape to other worlds filled with dragons, knights and princesses. She browsed the shelves for a grown version of that escape. She found a book she liked and as she was paying for the paperback, she noticed the Help Wanted sign.

"Are you still looking for help?" She asked the young lady ringing her up.

"Yes, are you interested?" The young lady, whose nametag read, Becca, asked enthusiastically.

"Yes, I am,"

"Hang on, let me get the owner." The young lady disappeared into the back.

A moment later she returned with a lady in her early sixties. "Hello, I'm Wendy I am the owner, Becca tells me you're looking for a job."

"Yes, ma'am, Blake Morgan and I just moved into town last week and I'm looking for work."

"Come back to the office; we'll talk a little more."

Blake smiled and followed Wendy into a small, but comfortable office with warm colors of burgundy and gold.

"Have a seat," Wendy pointed to an antique upholstered chair.

Blake sat down carefully.

"Where have you worked previously?" Wendy got straight to the point. Blake liked this woman already.

"I am a licensed architect. I've worked for the last ten years at Bergstrom and Bradley in Roanoke."

"An architect? Will you be teaching at the university?"

"I hope so, but I am still waiting to hear from them,"

Wendy nodded, "If you don't mind my asking, what made you decide to move all the way out to Gates Point?"

Blake had been dreading this question. She wanted to be honest without telling people she was a failure. That she had allowed a man to abuse her to the point of physical violence.

"I needed a change."

Wendy studied her for a moment. "If I needed to check references with your previous employer, what name would I use?"

"Townsend, Blake Townsend."

Wendy leaned back and smiled at Blake. "I understand, dear. Ever worked in retail before?"

"No," Blake suddenly wondered if she wasn't qualified to work in a bookstore. She didn't have any experience in retail, but she was sure she could learn. She suddenly needed this job; she couldn't handle another rejection right now. "I worked in fast food when I was in college." She blurted out.

"Close enough!" Wendy laughed, "When can you start?"

"How about tomorrow?"

"Welcome aboard." Wendy stood up and offered her hand to Blake.

"Thank you, can I ask one question?"

"Shoot," Wendy said.

"What is a bumboat?"

Wendy's laugh was infectious. "Have you ever been overseas to Asia or the islands?"

Blake shook her head, "No,"

"Well, in a lot of places where the larger boats can't make it all the way into port they have further away from the docks; so, the locals use smaller boats, bumboats, they call them to take their goods out to the larger boats to sell."

"I see," Blake smiled and left with the promise to return the next morning at ten o'clock. She walked to the market with a sense of accomplishment. She had a new apartment, a new name, a new job, and a renewed sense that everything was going to be alright.

CHAPTER THREE

"Logan, it's Friday night go home!" FBI Special Agent Ethan Craddock stood with his hands on his hips looking at his friend and co-worker.

"Yeah, okay boss, I'm going. I was just finishing up this report."

"I appreciate that, is it done?"

"Yes,"

"Then get out!"

Logan laughed, "Do you and Kay have plans for this weekend?"

"I think we might go fishing, want to join us?"

"No thanks, she takes her fishing too seriously for me."

Ethan laughed, remembering the first time Kay and Logan fished together. It had been early in Ethan and Kay's relationship, Ethan had brought Kay along on a fishing charter with Jared and Logan, things had been pretty tense for the first hour, but then Kay had challenged Logan to a contest to see who could catch the biggest fish and she won. They had started a friendship that day; it was slow to grow, but it had finally bloomed, and now Ethan wondered if Logan was more loyal to Kay than to him.

Ethan closed the office door behind them and called out to Logan as he headed for his car, "See you Monday."

Logan drove home, still wired up from the day. He walked to a local pub to see if any of the regulars were there tonight. As he walked past Bumboat Books, he noticed a woman behind the counter he hadn't seen before. He was familiar with everyone who worked there; it was ten minutes before the store would close. He would check to see if the most recent issue of Warrior's Weekly was out. He opened the door; a small brass bell alerted the woman to his presence. She looked up, as if the bell had startled her. The look of surprise quickly replaced by a pretty smile.

"Hello, can I help you find something in particular?"

"I was just checking for Warrior's Weekly,"

"Just came in today." She nodded towards the magazine rack, then focused on something else. He found the magazine and stood staring at the cover, then slowly flipped a few pages. Logan stole glances towards the counter. The woman appeared to be concentrating on something. She had rich auburn hair that under the soft glow of the bookstore lights reminded him of dark maple leaves in the fall. Her ice green eyes were a beautiful contrast to the warm color of her hair. He could tell she was aware of him. She kept her body turned so that she could see both him and the door. He wanted to talk to her, but her body language said she wanted people to keep their distance. He thought the fact it was closing time fueled her impatience. It was Friday night, after all. He walked over to the science fiction section and plucked a book off the shelf. He carried the book and magazine to where she stood.

"Did you find everything okay?"

"Yes, thank you," Logan noticed her eye contact was brief. "Are you new here? I don't remember seeing you before." She looked up at him puzzled and hesitated.

"Yes, just started."

"Oh, that's nice. My name is Logan, I'm sure I'll see you again, then." He smiled as he handed her cash. She eyed him suspiciously.

She handed him his change. "Thank you, have a pleasant weekend."

Logan ambled home slowly; the pub forgotten. He spent the rest of the night trying to forget those beautiful green eyes. He didn't want to think about the way she studied him. Why was he even thinking about her? Sure, she was beautiful, but he had no room in his life for that kind of distraction. He had watched his friend Ethan tear his guts out over Kay for years before they finally got together. The next morning, he decided he would go out for coffee; he told himself it was because the weather was nice for January and he wanted to enjoy it while it lasted. The wintry days of February would be here soon enough. He passed the bookstore on the opposite side of the street on his way to the coffee shop. He sat staring out the diner's window as shops began to open along Main Street as he drank his coffee, he spotted Wendy opening the bookstore.

She looked up at the sound of the brass bell, "Good morning, Logan."

"Morning, Wendy."

"Are you here for your magazine?"

"No, actually I got it last night. I noticed you had a new employee."

Wendy busied herself with preparing the store to open, "Oh yeah, you met Blake?"

"Yeah,"

"Isn't she a sweet one?" Wendy called over her shoulder as she was setting up a new display.

"Well, she doesn't talk much,"

"Oh, well, she's only been in town a few days, so she is still getting her bearings."

"Really? Where'd she come from?"

"Roanoke, I believe she is recovering from a nasty divorce and is trying to start over here."

"That would explain a lot." Logan thought about the vibe she was giving off. She wasn't just skeptical of strangers; she was skeptical of men. He certainly could understand her feelings.

"Was there something I could help you with this morning?" Wendy paused in her work.

"Oh no, I was just walking by, and thought I'd say hello." He started inching towards the door.

"Oh well, glad you did." Wendy suppressed a smile, "stop by anytime."

"Will do."

Logan drove northwest, out of the city to his weekend cottage. He needed to think about something other than Blake with the ice green eyes. He was just overworked. Fresh air and fishing would help clear his head.

By the time he reached his cabin, the temperatures were in the mid-fifties. Logan opened up the windows to get the fresh air moving through the cottage and grabbed a beer as he headed out to his small pier. He dropped a hook into the water and sat down to wait, his mind wondering back to Blake. He kept seeing those green eyes and that dark auburn hair.

***

Blake spent the morning unpacking the boxes of clothes and personal items she had brought with her. The apartment she rented came partially furnished, and she had ordered a mattress for the bed which was due to arrive the next day. She didn't have to be at work until two that afternoon. That gave her plenty of time to get her apartment organized and take stock of what else she needed. She liked Wendy, and thought she would enjoy working at the bookstore, but she was a little nervous every time the door opened, expecting to see Jerry coming through the door. He had gone from hurt and anger over to depression and back to anger. Portia's husband, Ted, made sure that the divorce decree stated Jerry was to not have any direct contact with Blake, any communication would go through him as her attorney. She hoped that Jerry would have enough sense to honor the terms of the divorce. Her cell phone rang, jarring her back to the present.

"Hello?"

"Hey Blake, how's it going?"

She sighed with relief at the sound of Portia's voice.

"Things are pretty good; I'm unpacking a few things this morning. I got a part-time job in a bookstore."

"Really, why?"

"I need something to do. I can't just sit around waiting for some epiphany about where I go from here."

"I get that, but why a bookstore?"

"It is a cool little place, pretty laid back, and I can walk to it from my apartment. The owner is really nice."

"As long as you're happy. So, what is Gates Point like? Is it as quaint as you imagined?"

"I haven't done much exploring. It is bigger than I imagined."

"That could be a good thing, more things to do." Portia was trying to be supportive.

"You should come visit. I live near the arts district there are all kinds of little shops and boutiques, you'd love it."

"I'll come visit so you can show me around and we can have a girl's weekend!"

Blake was excited at the thought of a girls' weekend with Portia. "Let me know when you're coming, I'll take time off from work. We'll have a blast."

"So, have you met any nice guys?" Portia finally got to her point.

"Portia, no! I want to figure out who I am. And I can't do that if I am someone's girlfriend, wife or anything else associated with a man."

"Not all relationships are like that. Besides, everyone knows the best part about a breakup is the rebound sex!"

Suddenly, images of the man in the bookstore flashed across her mind. What was his name? She was sure he had told her.

"Portia!"

"What? It's true just ask Meg and Amy. Ask anyone. No strings attached, just a good old fashion physical relationship."

"No, thanks."

"Don't be a prude, remember you're finding yourself, experimenting, trying new things you never tried before. Why not this?"

"Because I am not a tart! That's why."

"Blake, just promise me you'll loosen up and try to have a little fun."

"I promise." Blake crossed her fingers behind her back, even though Portia couldn't see her.

"Okay, gotta run. Have fun!"

"Bye, Portia." Blake clicked off and sat staring at her phone. Portia was right about one thing; she was on a journey of rediscovery. So far, she had managed to get a job and order a mattress. Not very exciting. She decided she would try harder. Blake needed some fresh air, so she walked down to the coffee shop and ordered an expensive coffee drink, Jerry would have said was a waste of money for something you could drink in five minutes. She was going to pay for it with Jerry's alimony money and enjoy every minute.

CHAPTER FOUR

It had been a week since starting the job at the bookstore, and Blake was feeling more confident about her new life. She had finished unpacking; treated herself to lunch and started a morning ritual of walking and grabbing a coffee on the way back to her apartment. Life was good.

Wendy came through the shop, turning off the lights. When she got to the front, Blake was still working on the inventory. "Blake, we are going out tonight for an end of the week destress drink, join us."

"Sure, I'll come along." Blake's heart skipped a beat. Her current lifestyle was exciting, and she was still adjusting.

"Awesome! We're going to go downtown for beer and pizza, that okay with you?"

"Sounds great."

Blake was a little self-conscious walking down the sidewalk. She kept looking around. It was irrational; there was no reason to think Jerry would look for her. He had not contacted her. She just needed to get over herself. Clearly, she never meant as much to him as he had meant to her at one time. She drew a deep breath.

Becca switched places with Wendy as they walked to Sal's pizza. "Hey Blake, have you ever been to Sal's?"

Blake smiled at Becca. "No, I'm looking forward to it, is it good?"

"It is the best, the family is first generation, the food is very authentic."

Blake appreciated Becca's youthful enthusiasm.

"That is awesome. What kind of pizza do you guys usually get?"

"We usually have to get two," she laughed, "because Wendy and Brad like anchovies and I don't. Do you like them?"

"No, not really."

Becca squealed, "Blake doesn't like anchovies either, I'm not outnumbered anymore!"

Brad, the other part-time employee and Wendy rolled their eyes. "You two are missing out!" Brad announced.

Becca squeezed Blake's arm, "Tell me please you like white pizza!"

Blake couldn't help but laugh along with Becca, "I do."

"Yes! Finally, I have found my pizza soul mate. Her name is Blake!"

The four of them laughed and linked arms as they strolled past a few other pubs and restaurants before arriving at Sal's Pizzeria.

Logan was sitting near the window inside the Sunset Sports bar with Jared and Ethan. They were celebrating the closing of a case; with no recent cases the coming week promised a calmer case load. The sound of laughter drew Logan's attention to the scene outside the window when he saw Blake walking by. She was with Wendy and the other bookstore employees. He turned in his chair for a better view, but the angle was wrong, and he couldn't see where she was going.

"Logan is everything alright?" Ethan asked.

"What?"

"Everything alright over there?"

"Oh yeah, fine."

Logan feigned interest in his beer. Jared and Ethan exchange looks. "See someone you recognized?" Jared pressed.

"No."

Jared shrugged and flagged a server for another round. "What do you say we order some wings?" Jared looked at his friends.

"Yeah, sure" Logan and Ethan agreed. The server nodded and left, only to return a few moments later. "Here's your beer and your wings will be out shortly."

Jared nodded, "Thanks."

Ethan studied Logan. They had worked together a long time; and were close. Close enough that Ethan could tell when something was bothering Logan and tonight his friend was suddenly on edge. He had seen something on the street, Ethan was sure of it.

The wings came and Logan seemed to relax again. He looked at Ethan, "So why isn't Stephanie joining us tonight?"

Jared wiped his mouth, "She is having a girl's night or something."

Logan nodded. He needed to distract Ethan; to focus the attention away from himself. "Who's watching the game tomorrow night?"

Ethan shook his head, "Not me, Kay and I have other plans." Jared looked at Ethan in surprise, "Really? I thought Kay was a bigger sports fan than all of us combined."

Logan chuckled, "her team sucks this year." Ethan laughed, "Pretty much."

With the wings cleared away, Logan's turned his attention back to the window like he was expecting to see something or someone.

Finally, Jared flagged the server for their bill, "I'd better call it a night."

"Yeah, me too," Ethan agreed, "You okay to get home, Jared?"

"Yeah, I'm fine, but I'm not so sure about the big guy." He nodded towards Logan.

"Don't worry about him, I'll handle it,"

"You sure?"

"Yeah, see you Monday,"

Jared nodded and left. Ethan turned his attention to Logan, "What's eating you?"

Logan frowned, "Nothing!"

"Uh huh, come on, I'll drive you home."

"I can manage,"

"I'm sure you can, but it's not an option, so let's go."

There was no use in arguing with Ethan, so he got up and staggered out of the bar. When they arrived at Logan's place in town, Ethan got out of the car to help his friend.

"This isn't our first date; you don't have to walk me to the door." Logan joked.

"I'm coming in with you."

Logan nodded; Ethan would not let the subject drop. He sighed heavily, "Come on, then." He unlocked the door and walked in, leaving Ethan to follow him, "You want another beer, or would you rather have coffee?"

"Neither thanks."

Logan faced Ethan, "Okay let's have it."

"Tell me, what's on your mind tonight? What did you see on the street that had you pounding a few more beers than normal?"

"It's nothing."

Ethan crossed his arms, "I'm not leaving until you tell me."

Logan narrowed his gaze. There was no doubt he had too much to drink because he was wondering if he could take Ethan in his current condition. It would be a close match if they have got physical, but Ethan was his best friend, he would not fight with him.

Ethan relaxed a bit, "What's her name?" He chuckled at the look on Logan's face. "Don't give me that look, I've been where you are right now, and you asked me the same question."

Logan ran his hand over his hair.

"Fine," He looked around the room, trying to decide how to explain to Ethan that he knew nothing about this woman and yet he couldn't stop thinking about her. "All I know is that her name is Blake, she is new in town and works at the bookstore."

"Well, that's a pretty good start. How did you meet her?"

"I stopped in the bookstore. And she was there."

"And you two struck up a conversation?"

"No, just the opposite, I tried, but she wasn't having it. She barely looked at me and said the bare minimum to get me checked out."

"Interesting."

"I thought so too, I returned the next day and talked to Wendy Harvey, the owner. Wendy told me she just moved here from the valley and that she must have gone through a terrible break up there."

"Okay, so why were you looking for her on the sidewalk last night?"

"I don't know, I mean she's got the most incredible eyes."

"Yes," Ethan said, thinking about how he still got lost in Kay's eyes. "Yes, I am very familiar with the effects of a beautiful woman's eyes."

"And she had this dark auburn hair like maple leaves in the fall."

Ethan laughed.

"What's so funny?"

"You've got it bad." Ethan laughed again.

"It's crazy, she wouldn't give me the time of day, and I can't get her out of my head!" Logan's hands clenched into fists. "What do I do about it?"

"Well, you only have two options. First, you can just forget it, find something else to think about,"

Logan scowled at Ethan, "The second option?"

"Go back to the bookstore. Talk to her, get to know her and let her find out what a great guy you are."

Logan snorted a laugh. "Yeah, easier said than done."

"Do you want to wait six years, like I did?"

"No, I don't want any part of what you went through, brother."

"No, you don't," Ethan put a hand on Logan's shoulder "Tomorrow find a reason to go in there and talk to her." He turned to leave.

"Ethan?"

"Yeah, big guy?"

"I'm scared. And that has me messed up."

"Yeah, that is part of it, too. But you'll be alright." Ethan smiled, "speaking of scary, I'm going home before Kay wonders where I am."

Logan laughed. "I wouldn't want her mad at me. You better go. And Ethan, Thanks."

"No problem."

Logan stood rooted in place for several long minutes after Ethan left, thinking about going back to the bookstore. The thought thrilled him and terrified him.

CHAPTER FIVE

Blake and her co-workers sat at a large booth sharing pizza and beers. She smiled to herself knowing in that moment she would be okay; she couldn't worry about things beyond her control. Blake was ready to restart her life and forget the past. The summer semester at Batten University wouldn't be starting for three and a half months, giving her plenty of time to explore her new city, and herself before embarking on a new career. She decided tomorrow morning she would go to the seawall for an early morning walk and enjoy the sunrise over the water. She would start living like a normal person again.

***

Logan took an ibuprofen before going to bed, hoping to ward off the headache that comes from eating too little and drinking too much. Ethan's words replayed themselves over and over as he was waiting for sleep to come.

Despite the going to bed late and drunk, Logan still woke up early, took a bracing shower and dressed for a run along the seawall to clear the cobwebs from his head. He drove to the old fort; parked at the north end and stretched. He took in the early morning view of the Chesapeake Bay, before starting off on his five-mile run. He needed to concentrate and keep his mind free of distractions. He got to the two-and-a-half-mile mark and despite his fierce concentration, something caught his eye. A woman sitting on a bench along the seawall, staring at the water. He came to a halt even from the back he recognized that dark auburn hair shown morning light like a beacon belonged to Blake. Indecision plagued him; should he walk up and say hello, how creepy was that? But if he kept going, and she saw him? Would she think he was rude for not speaking? Did she care either way? He put his hands on his hips and bent over; he needed to get it together. As he was straightening up, she turned and saw him. He feigned surprise.

"Hello,"

She studied him for a minute as if she was trying to place him.

"Hello," She answered.

"It's Blake, right? From the bookstore?"

"Yes, that's right. You're Logan, who likes science fiction." She smiled at him and his heart melted completely. He grinned like an idiot that she remembered his name and what he liked to read.

"It's a beautiful morning." He stated the obvious, not knowing what else to say.

She looked out at the water, "It is so beautiful here, I love the way the air smells."

Logan smiled and nodded as she spoke, hanging on her every word "I understand what you mean, its why I like to come out here in the mornings. The view is fantastic, and nothing cures you like the salt air."

"Are you from here?"

He noticed her posture was more relaxed today than in the store. "No, but I've lived here for about ten years."

She looked up at him. "Where else have you lived and what made you decide to live here?"

He looked down at the bench, "Do you mind?" He pointed.

"Oh, I'm so sorry, please sit down."

Logan sat down, but not too close. "I was in the military, so I've moved around a lot."

"Oh, I see." She looked down for a moment. "Where did you grow up?"

"A little place in the Tennessee mountains you've never heard of."

She nodded.

"What about you?" He asked.

"I grew up in Roanoke,"

"What brought you here?"

She looked pensive. "I was ready for a change. I read an article in a garden magazine about Gates Point and I thought, it was just as good a place as any to start over."

Logan nodded, "I get that."

Blake smiled at him and seemed to relax. "What do you do?"

Logan looked at her, trying to gauge her reaction before he spoke.

"For a living?" Blake clarified.

"Oh, sorry. I work for the FBI."

Blakes eyes widened, "Really?"

Logan chuckled at her response. "Yeah,"

"So, like an agent or an analyst?"

"Field Agent."

"That sounds exciting." She beamed.

"It's not like TV."

"I hope not," she laughed.

The conversation lulled for a moment; Logan found he didn't want it to end. "Have you had breakfast yet?"

"No,"

"Let me buy you breakfast?" He asked, holding his breath while waiting for the answer.

She hesitated but finally relented. "Yeah, okay."

Logan's heart leapt in his throat. "Okay, did you drive here?"

Blake nodded, "Yes,"

"Me too. How about Colonial Pancakes over on Wine Street? I'll meet you there?"

Blake breathed a sigh of relief that he didn't suggest that they ride together. She smiled, "I'll see you there."

She arrived first; she sat in the car, second guessing her decision. Just as she had almost convinced herself that this was a mistake, Logan pulled up in a huge pickup truck and parked a couple of spots away from her. He said he was an FBI agent; they have background checks, right? He couldn't be a psychopath. She blew out a breath and got out of the car.

Logan smiled and held the door open for her. A sign greeted them "Seat Yourself" Logan chose a booth upfront next to a window. He wasn't trying to force her into seclusion and hide her away like Jerry used to do when they would go out, almost like it embarrassed him to be seen with her. But she had learned he was cheating on her with every willing woman in Roanoke, and he probably didn't want to run into any of them. She pushed thoughts of her past aside and concentrated on Logan. She liked that she could see the door and her car if she decided she wanted to leave. It made her feel safe and in control. Colonial Pancakes was in an old brick building, but it had lots of windows it gave it an open and airy atmosphere. Everything inside was yellow and white, from the walls to the server's uniforms. There were black and white photographs of the building in its previous life, along the walls and items that Blake guessed were historic memorabilia from days long past.

"Coffee?" A server interrupted her thoughts.

"Yes, please." She nodded as the server set down two mugs and began pouring.

"I'll be back in a minute to take your order."

Logan nudged the cream and sugar towards her. She added a little of both. He drank his black.

"So," Logan suddenly had the urge to break the silence, "Do you enjoy working in the bookstore?"

"Yes, Wendy is a wonderful person. She hired me with no retail experience except for when I was in college. But I really needed the job."

"Wendy is a very kind person. What do you do for a living, besides work at the bookstore?"

"I am an architect, and I will start teaching in the summer semester,"

"You'll leave the bookstore?"

"Not if I can help it. Wendy needs the help and I really enjoy it; it will mostly depend on my teaching schedule and workload."

Logan nodded his understanding and sipped more coffee.

"What about you? How long have you been an agent?"

"About twelve years, ten of them here in the Gates Point field office."

It was Blake's turn to nod. "What made you want to work for the FBI?"

"Well, I'm not the sort of person who can sit at a desk and crunch numbers all day. My military training gave me the skills to work in some sort of law enforcement."

"But why the FBI? Why not the local police or U.S. Marshalls?" She knew little about either and was curious what made a person choose what seemed like an extremely dangerous profession.

Logan couldn't help but smile, "I couldn't see myself walking a beat in uniform or riding one of those bicycles around the mall parking lot, so I decided the local police wasn't really an option. I applied to the Marshall service, but the FBI offered me a job first and the rest, as they say, is history."

The server reappeared.

"What would you like to order?" She said with her pencil posed over a pad suggesting that 'no' was not an option.

Blake smiled up at her, "I'll have the garden omelet with wheat toast."

"And you, sir?"

"The Denver omelet with hash browns."

"You said you saw an article in a magazine about Gates Point, did you leave Roanoke for the job at the college?"

"No," Blake paused, "I was just coming out of a nasty divorce and I needed a change of scenery." There she said it out loud to a virtual stranger she was a divorcee. She wondered if Logan would still be interested in sitting here with her. It was the twenty-first century; would he think she couldn't get her life together or couldn't manage a relationship? Instead, he looked at her with kindness in his eyes.

"I'm sorry to hear that. I hope things will be better for you here."

Blake studied his face. She believed him. He seemed sincere, and she was happy to find acceptance where she had been expecting rejection.

The server returned with their food, "Here you are,"

They discussed their favorite books and authors over breakfast. Blake hardly noticed the plates being cleared away. When the bill arrived, Logan deftly slid it to his side of the table before Blake could grab it or protest.

"Thank you," Blake offered. "For breakfast."

Logan smiled, "Anytime," his phone buzzed in his pocket. "Excuse me,"

Blake sat back and looked out the window to offer him privacy.

He clicked his phone, "Yeah?"

"Logan, it's Ethan, you busy?"

"A little,"

"Sorry about that, but we have a case, I need you at the office."

"I was out jogging; I need to change."

"Make it quick."

Logan clicked off. "I'm sorry, it's work, I have to go."

"It's okay, I understand." Blake slid from the booth and Logan followed.

Blake turned to Logan when she reached her car. "Thank you again,"

"My pleasure, it can be tough getting your bearings in a new town. If you need anything, just call me." He handed her his business card. "My cell number is at the bottom, use it." He winked at her.

She giggled just a little, "Okay, I will."

"I've gotta run," He apologized moving towards his truck, "I'll see again at the store!"

She waved and watched him pull out of the lot. It was nice to have a friend all her own. Just for her. She looked down at his card and read the name and number. She tucked it in her wallet and drove home.

CHAPTER SIX

Logan sped home for a quick shower and a change of clothes. Whatever case they had going on, it would not ruin his day. He would walk on clouds the rest of the week after sitting with Blake.

Logan came bursting through the door. "I'm here, boss!"

"'bout time." Jared teased.

"It's called exercise, try it sometime." Logan cut a glare at Jared.

"No thanks, I'm young enough to stay in shape without having to kill myself by running around with a pack on. That's just crazy."

"I wasn't wearing a pack and one day you're going to wish...,"

Ethan turned on the two of them. "Both of you knock it off, we have work to do." The room fell silent.

"You're right, boss, sorry." Logan turned his attention to Ethan. "What do we have?"

"Potential sighting of Thomas Wayne Moore, over on the 5th Street Pier." Ethan clicked the remote and brought the overhead screen alive with a mug shot and details of the charges pending against Moore.

"I'm not familiar with this one," Jared stood studying the screen.

Agent Stephanie Fisher spoke up. "He's wanted in connection with the death of his two children and wife. He shot them and then blew up the house to cover up the murders."

"Holy hell," Jared looked from the screen to Stephanie, "how long ago?"

"Ten years ago, in Texas,"

"And someone thinks they saw him here?" Jared was skeptical.

"Yes, one of our regular informants, claims to have seen him buying bait at the pier." Ethan added.

Logan was ready to charge out the door. "Is he still there?"

"No, but they say he comes nearly every day to fish. So, we stake the place out and see if he shows up." Ethan, advised.

"On it," Logan grabbed his backpack to make sure he had everything he needed. Jared and Stephanie checked their packs as well.

"Okay, check the trucks make sure we have everything we need for surveillance and a quick takedown." Ethan removed his government issued 9mm handgun from the locked desk drawer and grabbed the keys to one of the Chevy suburban's out in the parking lot.

They stopped a few blocks away from the pier and parked behind a convenience store.

Ethan looked around, "Logan scout out a couple of vantage points for us, we'll wait here."

Logan walked to the edge of the lot, turned east up the street in the direction of the fishing pier. He keyed his radio.

"Boss, if you turn right out of the parking lot come to the end of the street there is a wide alley behind some apartments. The apartment roof is a perfect place for a spotter. It gives us a view of the pier itself."

"Okay, Stephanie, I want you on the roof." Ethan said into the radio.

"You got it."

Jared drove the suburban to the alley, while Logan moved out to find another vantage point to the north that would give them a view of the private road leading to the pier.

"Boss, there is a spot over here on First Street. It isn't ideal, nothing higher than one story, but we can park next to a service garage and see the approach to the pier and then pull in behind him as he comes in if we need to."

"On my way," Ethan drove to Logan's location and backed the truck in next to Little Joe's auto repair.

Logan jumped in next to Ethan. "Okay, I didn't see a car matching the description of our guy in the parking lot."

"Are we close enough for you to see when him on the pier in case the car description is accurate?" Ethan asked.

Logan pulled his camera from the bag and attached the telephoto lens. "I can't see him from here, he could be on the other side."

Ethan keyed his mic, "Stephanie, do you have your camera with you?"

"Yes, I have it,"

"Can you look for Moore?"

"Got it."

Stephanie repeated Logan's steps and focused on the south side of the pier. She scanned the pier for several minutes. "I don't see him, boss."

"Okay, keep your eyes open."

They sat watching the pier and the for the next eight hours. Finally, Ethan called off the surveillance.

"Either our boy doesn't need to fish today, or we're blown. Let's call it a night and we'll try again tomorrow."

"Copy that," Stephanie slid back down the exterior wall of the apartment building to the fire escape and stretched. Jared came around the corner to pick her up.

"Thank god the boss shut us down for the night, I'm starving."

Stephanie rolled her eyes, "You're always starving."

"Because I'm always working and not being fed."

Stephanie shook her head at Jared's constant griping. "Get in the truck."

The team met back at the office; Ethan's frustration showed.

"Bet I don't get to go eat now either," Jared whispered to Stephanie when Ethan and Logan came in behind them.

"Okay, so things didn't pan out today, but we'll go back tomorrow," Ethan stood in the middle of the office. Logan sat down and leaned back in his chair, making it squeak loudly.

"Tomorrow morning, Jared and Stephanie, you take the first shift."

"Sounds good," Jared leaned forward hoping to leave soon he was eager to agree to anything that started tomorrow. "What time?"

"Look at a tide chart," Logan bellowed, "When the tide is coming in, that is when you watch for him."

"I know about tide charts!" Jared sniped back.

"Chill out! Both of you." Ethan held up his hands to diffuse the situation before it got out of control.

Logan shook his head and muttered. "So dense sometimes."

"What did you say?" Jared jumped up from his desk.

Logan slowly leaned forward, his chair back in the upright position.

"Go home!" Ethan grabbed Jared by the shoulders.

"But he's always has something smart-ass to say."

"Did you hear what he said just now?" Ethan stood so Jared couldn't see Logan.

"No,"

"Then chill out."

"Come on Jared, I'll buy you a pizza." Stephanie offered, trying to distract Jared with the promise of food. She looked over at Ethan, "He gets cranky when he's hungry." Stephanie grabbed Jared by the arm, "Let's go."

"What kind of pizza?"

"Any kind you want just come on before you get yourself into trouble."

Jared reluctantly followed Stephanie out the door.

Ethan waited until Jared and Stephanie were out of the office before turning to Logan. "What have I told you about winding him up like that?"

"And I told you he is a punk kid who knows nothing. He is too cocky, and he needs to be open to learning before he gets himself or one of us hurt."

"He wouldn't be part of this team if he wasn't good enough. So, lay off!"

Logan stood up, "Why are you always protecting him?"

"I wouldn't have to, if you'd lay off. What is your problem?"

"Nothing!"

"Is this about that girl?"

"No!"

Ethan paused at the force of Logan's denial. It was about the girl. "Listen to me, Logan, and listen carefully. It's easy to have someone consume you. You need to accept how you feel about her and deal with it. You can't bottle that stuff up; trust me, I've been there and back."

Logan drew in a deep breath, staring up at the ceiling for a moment. Ethan was right; hadn't he watched Ethan nearly come apart over Kay. Ethan had fallen in love with Kay at first sight, but the timing was all wrong. Ethan lived with his feelings locked away until he saw Kay again. During those six years, Ethan divorced his wife, allowing himself to come to terms with his feelings. Now, they were living together happily, and Ethan was a changed man. Logan didn't have the complications Ethan and Kay had, but Blake wasn't ready for a relationship. He refused to push her into something, only to lose her. Logan wasn't really sure about his own feelings at the moment: they were equal parts love and fear. He exhaled.

"You're right,"

Ethan's smile was met with a typical Logan scowl.

"Wipe that look off your face, its complicated."

Ethan kept his smile, "It always is in relationships. Why don't you go home?"

"Yeah, great, it's that simple just go home." Logan headed for the door.

"Then go see her."

Logan looked back at Ethan and shook his head. But decided not to explain the situation any further. He walked to his truck and paused before getting in. He would go see her except it was late, and the bookstore was closed, but he could at least drive by it on his way home. That might ease some tension.

***

It had been a long day at the store, Blake walked home more feeling more tired than she had in a long time. But it wasn't the. If she was honest, she had expected to see Logan today. She got her hopes up every time the door opened and then dashed when it wasn't him. Then she got angry with herself for letting her emotions get tangled up over a man. What was wrong with her? Was she a glutton for punishment? She just got rid of one controlling man in her life. Why was she so eager to jump into another relationship? No, she needed to find herself first. She couldn't allow herself to lose her identity again. Blake had to make sure she knew who she was, before giving herself over to another man. The microwave announced her dinner was ready, pulling her back to reality. Sitting at home alone on the on the sofa eating microwave meals alone in front of the TV, wasn't her idea of success in her journey of self-discovery.

CHAPTER SEVEN

Wendy came into the bookstore from the rear employees' entrance. The lights were on in the back, which meant Blake must be there. Wendy had had doubts about hiring Blake. She had little retail experience, but Wendy could see she needed something to help her get grounded in a new city. Blake worked harder than anyone else. She wondered how much that would change in a couple of weeks when Blake started teaching part time. She hated to lose her, but she would understand if Blake quit altogether. "Good Morning, Blake!"

"Good Morning, I'm up front!"

Wendy smelled fresh coffee and found Blake in the science fiction section stocking a new shipment of used books that had arrived the day before.

"You're here early."

"Hi Wendy, yeah. I couldn't sleep, so I thought I'd get a head start on entering these in the computer and on the shelves."

"I appreciate that, but what will the other employees do?"

Blake looked up, dejected.

"I'm only joking, I really appreciate the hard work, this place runs so much better with you here."

Blake smiled, "Thanks."

Wendy noticed that there was still something under the surface of Blake and made her seem sad. Blake had been at the bookstore a month now, and she had come out of her shell, but there still seemed to be something haunting her. "Is everything alright?"

"What?" Blake looked up; surprised Wendy was still standing there. "No, no, I'm fine."

Wendy could see she wasn't. "Why don't you take a break and come have some coffee with me? We have an hour before the store opens, let's chat." Wendy turned and walked away so that Blake couldn't argue. She poured two cups of coffee and suggested they sit in the chairs in the makeshift break room.

"So, tell me, how is everything going? You settled in, okay?"

"Oh yeah, even bought a house plant and everything."

"Houseplants are brilliant conversationalist." Wendy quipped, "What about friends?"

"I have you guys."

"Yes, you do. We are all here for you. But we don't go out that often. How much time do you hang out with us or friends outside of the bookstore?"

Blake simply shrugged. "I talk with my friend Portia from back home about once a week."

Wendy pressed on, "That's good, but she is there and you're here. You need a support system here. Are you close to anyone in Gates Point?"

Blake thought about Logan. "Not really, other than you."

Wendy shook her head sadly, "Really? What's my cat's name?"

Blake looked at Wendy, perplexed for a moment. She knew where Wendy was going with this conversation and she wasn't wrong.

"I didn't know you had a cat."

Wendy laughed, "Don't all bookstore owners have cats?"

"I wouldn't think so, necessarily."

Wendy laughed, "you are too logical for your own good. I don't have a cat, that is not the point."

Blake sighed, "Your point is I need to get out more."

"Yes, you do. I just don't understand why you don't. Are you afraid of something? You don't strike me as overly introverted when you talk to the customers,"

"Oh Ms. Greenly, has a cat." Blake laughed.

"The customers are not a substitute for friends." Wendy shook her head.

"I'm sorry, is that a problem?" Blake asked.

"No, it's not a problem if you're an introvert. But I don't think you are introverted. I think there is something troubling you that is causing you to hold back from making new friends. There are five people in this store who are ready and willing to be a friend to you, if you let them."

Blake's shoulders slumped.

"I guess, I just have developed trust issues since being married to Jerry."

"Honey, there is nothing on this planet that will cause you to distrust people like someone who steals your heart and throws it away. If you let that man's action dictate how you live now and who you trust, then he still has his hooks in you."

Blake sat stunned at Wendy's words. Wendy was right, of course, but why hadn't she seen it before now. "You're exactly right! I've been trying to move past it and telling myself I had, but I guess I haven't moved on completely."

Wendy nodded, "I've been there. Now, let's talk about that young man that comes in here to see you."

Blake feigned surprise. "Who?" she stalled. But her heart did a flip and the butterflies in her stomach woke up at the hint of Logan.

Wendy scowled, "You know darn well, I'm talking about Logan Watson."

"How do you know him?"

"He's been coming in here for a few years. We chat once in a while."

Blake's heart sank, so he wasn't coming in to see her, he was just a regular customer. One that was hot as hell. But still just a regular.

"Oh,"

"And in all the time he's never looked at anyone else the way he looks at you, and believe me, I don't think he has ever said more than two words to anyone else."

Blake's heart lifted a little. "Really?"

Wendy laughed, "Yeah, really. You like him, don't you?"

"I do. But I'm not sure I should."

"Why?"

"Because I've been divorced only a short time. I shouldn't be too eager to jump into another relationship."

"That makes sense, you want to make sure your secure in your own identity before you can share a part of yourself with someone else. I understand, just don't let that cause you to miss an opportunity to get to know someone like Logan. Have you told him at all how you feel?"

"No!"

"Has he told you he has feelings for you?"

"Not really, I mean, I think he likes me well enough. We went out to breakfast last week, but I haven't seen him since then..." Blake shrugged her shoulders.

"You went for breakfast? That's great."

"Yeah, we sort of ran into each other out at the old fort, then he invited me to coffee and breakfast, and we talked for a while, but then he got called into work."

"Did he tell you he works for the FBI?"

"Yeah, he did."

"Well, he is probably busy with a case or something."

"Yeah, but I didn't give him my number or anything, so he doesn't really have a way to contact me, anyway."

Wendy studied Blake's face; she empathized. Blake was clearly conflicted about Logan and relationships. But Wendy knew Logan well enough to be sure that given the chance, he could help Blake heal.

"Well, he works for the FBI, he will find you." Wendy laughed and patted Blake's arm. "Now we better open the store."

"Oh my gosh, we've been talking for an hour!" Blake jumped up.

"I'll get the door." Wendy smiled.

"Okay, I'll go finish shelving those books before someone trips over them."

Blake returned to her pile of books and sat down on the floor to reach the lower shelves. She had chosen to work on the science fiction books because that was the genre that Logan liked and because she was avoiding the romance section. Valentine's Day was just a week away. She and Jerry had never celebrated it because to Jerry it was just a gimmick for retailers to suck you in and take your money. It still stung to think she would be alone on the most romantic day of the year. She wondered if Portia and the girls would come visit her that weekend. She was thinking about what Wendy had said, and it all made perfect sense. The only rules she needed to worry about now were her own. She was free to live her life on her own terms. If she was interested in Logan, that was okay. It didn't matter what anyone else thought.

"Hi,"

A deep voice snapped her back to reality. She looked up to see Logan smiling down at her.

"Uh, oh. Hi," she struggled to get to her feet, suddenly clumsy as a schoolgirl.

Logan reached out to steady her, "Here, let me help you,"

Blake blushed, "Thank you."

"What are you doing?"

"We got some new books, so I was just getting them on the shelves." Blake dusted herself off. "Were you looking for something new?"

Logan smiled and shook his head, "No, I came by to see you."

Blake felt the heat rising in her face, "Me?"

"Yeah, after we had coffee the other day, I thought I would have time to get together again before now, but work has been kind of hectic." It was Logan's turn to look uncomfortable.

"I see," She suppressed a smile. Wendy had been right.

"Uh, well, I still have to go to work, but wanted to stop by and tell you I enjoyed having coffee with you the other day."

Blake blushed, "I enjoyed it too,"

"I was wondering, if you wanted to, we could get together... again." His voice trailed as he stumbled over the words.

"Yeah, that would be nice."

"Yeah?" Logan looked like it surprised him she said yes. "You like to fish?"

"I've never tried it."

"Really? Well, okay, then I can teach you this weekend."

"That sounds like fun."

"Okay, well, I'd better go. Oh, uh, can I call you to give you the details later?"

"Sure," Blake pulled a bookmark she had found in a book and wrote her phone number on the back.

Logan looked at the number. "Okay, I'll call you soon." He started walking backwards down the row of books. Blake followed him.

"Okay, bye." She waved as he left.

Wendy stood shamelessly, watching. She beamed when Blake caught her in mid stare. "Good for you, girly!" Wendy laughed.

Blake smiled to herself, "Yeah, good for me."

***

Ethan looked up from his computer as Logan came through the office door, "Where've you been?"

"Ethan, I had to run an errand, okay?"

"Yeah, man." Ethan studied Logan carefully. He pushed back from his desk and stood up to stretch. Logan looked like a man on the edge. "Listen, why don't you take the night off, you look a little strung out."

Logan wheeled around to face Ethan, "I am not taking a night off and leave you shorthanded in the middle of an investigation."

Ethan raised his hands, "Hey, Logan, man. What's going on with you?"

"Sorry." Logan hung his head and turned away.

Ethan lowered his hands but stayed rooted in the same spot, "If you want to talk about it, I'm here, but listen. I need you focused on this case, okay?"

Logan turned back around to face Ethan, "Yeah, I'm sorry. I'm all in, boss."

"You sure?"

Logan nodded, he needed to pull it together. What was he freaking out about? He had a date to teach a girl to fish. That was hardly anything to stress about. He had been on plenty of dates in his life. This was no big deal.

"I'm here, boss, one hundred percent."

Ethan smiled, "Okay, then let's go relieve Jared and Stephanie. He's probably eaten his weight in roller food by now."

Jared seemed to be perpetually hungry.

Ethan called Stephanie on her cell.

"Hi boss,"

"Hey Logan and I are on our way, any luck?"

"Not yet. The tide is still coming in, so he might still show up. Jared says the blue fish are biting."

"How does he know that?"

"He was talking to one of the guys in the snack bar when he bought his fourth hot dog."

Ethan winced, there was a time when he could eat like Jared, but not anymore. Getting old was a bitch.

"Okay, well we are leaving now, be there soon." Ethan clicked off.

"Any luck out there?"

"No, but Jared has eaten four snack bar hot dogs."

"Uh! Glad Stephanie is sitting with him instead of me."

They both laughed and drove down to the pier.

They were nearly there when Stephanie called back. Logan answered.

"Logan here,"

"Logan, he's here, just pulled in and is getting his fishing gear out of the trunk of his car."

Logan put the phone on speaker and relayed the information to Ethan.

"Okay, Stephanie. Jared, I want you to keep eyes on, but to not engage. We will be there in five."

"Boss, Jared is out of the truck."

"Where is he?"

"Guess."

"Up on the pier?"

"Yeah,"

"We are nearly there you wait for us!" Ethan gunned the gas.

Logan was shaking his head. He had the truck door open before Ethan came to a complete stop. Stephanie met them in the parking lot of the pier.

"Any sign of Jared yet?"

"No, and Moore is buying bait. If he doesn't hurry, Jared is going to walk right into him."

Logan gave Ethan a look that said he was ready to shake some sense into Jared.

"Let's go in slow, we don't need to spook him. We also don't want any innocents getting caught up in this." Ethan instructed. Logan kept his gun down by his side, helping to conceal it. "Logan, you go in first, carefully and tell me what you see. Try to get Jared's attention."

"You got it."

Ethan and Stephanie flanked the entrance to the snack bar and bait shop at the base of the pier. Their suspect was standing at the counter to the right, Jared was in the men's room to the left and Logan was casually strolling up the middle.

"Can I help you, sir?" The man behind the counter called to Logan as Moore moved away.

"No, thanks just looking for a friend."

Moore took his cup of worms and walked out onto the pier without giving Logan a second look. Jared came out of the men's room, saw Moore, hesitated, and then he saw Logan. He crouched and drew his sidearm and shouted. "FBI, freeze!"

"Shit!" Ethan and Stephanie ran in behind Logan, who was moving to flank Moore as he dropped his gear and pulled a fileting knife from his belt. He sprinted further out onto the pier and grabbed a young boy fishing with his dad and put the knife to his throat.

He was holding the boy close and dragging him backwards down the pier. People were scrambling to get out of the way. Many were reaching for their cell phones.

"Stay back or I'll cut him, I swear!"

Ethan advanced on Moore, "It doesn't have to happen like this, we don't want to hurt you, we just need to talk to you, I think you know that."

"I know I'm not going to jail!"

"Boss," Logan growled, he raised his gun he had a clear shot of Moore's head, and was ready to shoot to save the boy.

Ethan looked over and saw Logan was taking aim.

"Not here, too many civilians, too risky."

"Tommy Wayne Moore, you are coming with us so make it easy on yourself." Ethan called out again. Ethan could see that Moore wasn't planning on coming peacefully. Instead, he was making his way to the end of the pier where the water was deep. He was going to jump, Ethan knew it. He just needed to keep him from hurting the boy first.

Stephanie and Jared were following Ethan and clearing people off the pier as they went, most of them were taking video as the team advanced on Moore who was still pressing the knife to the boy's throat.

"Stay back!" Moore was desperate, he knew they had him cornered, and he would not go to jail. He knew how they treated people who killed children in prison.

"This doesn't have to end this way!" Ethan continued. Then quietly, he spoke to Logan, "You got him if he goes over?"

"Yeah, boss."

Ethan advanced on Moore, hoping he would soon let the boy go. "You don't want to hurt that boy, do you?"

"I will if you don't stay back!"

"I'm back, but I have to keep close enough to help that boy if you hurt him."

"You don't care about him, you'll jump me!"

"I will not harm you at all Tommy, you see my friend over there?" He nodded towards Logan.

"Yeah."

"You hurt that boy he's going to shoot you, no questions asked. And I'm here to give that boy first aid, so you see you just need to let the boy go and you can live through this."

The boy was panicking. He was panting, and his eyes were wide and moving from side to side.

"Son, look at me." Ethan moved to get the boy's attention. "Look only at me, I'm Agent Craddock and I'm going to make sure you go home safely today, do you understand?"

The boy locked eyes with Ethan and nodded.

"That's right, just keep looking at me, don't take your eyes off of me, okay?"

The boy nodded again.

"What's your name?"

"Corey."

"Okay, good. Thank you, Corey. Now you just keep your eyes focused on me and don't worry about the man behind you."

"He, he has a knife!"

"I know he does, Corey, but you see my friend over there. He has a gun, and we will let nothing happen to you, I promise."

The boy nodded.

"You're going to shoot me!" Moore yelled.

"My buddy, there is a former Special Forces sniper, and he could have taken your ass out ten minutes ago. I told you Tommy; don't "We don't want anyone to get hurt today. Not you and not this little boy. So put the knife down and we can all walk away from this."

"Boss?" Stephanie crept up behind Ethan, opposite Logan.

"Trust me." Ethan answered her unspoken question. He knew his team was thinking why not just shoot Moore in the head, but the knife was dangerously close to the boy's throat and Ethan was afraid that even if Logan shot him, the knife would still cut Corey.

They reached the end of the pier and Moore had nowhere else to go.

"Last chance, let the boy go!"

"You want him? Come and get him!" Moore shoved the boy to Ethan and jumped over the railing into the water. Ethan grabbed Corey. Logan sprinted and dove over the rail into the black water after Moore. Stephanie ran to the rail just as Logan disappeared below the surface.

"Jared, get the EMT's up here now!" Jared waved to the EMT's that had arrived just ahead of the news crews.

"Corey, you did good today, you were very brave." Ethan ruffled his hair as the EMT's wrapped him in a blanket and walked him down the pier to his father and the ambulance.

"Has he come up yet?" Ethan rushed to the rail.

"Not yet!"

Jared, Stephanie and Ethan walked along the pier looking for Logan to pop up out of the water. The lights on the pier made it hard to see anything in the water. Ethan was getting worried when Jared called out.

"There! Near the beach!"

The trio sprinted down the pier and met Logan on the water's edge. He drug Moore up onto the sand and dropped him hand cuffed at Ethan's feet. "Got him, boss."

Ethan chuckled and shook his head.

"Good job."

Ethan turned to Jared, "pick him up and finish what you started."

Jared could see that Ethan wasn't happy with him. He lifted Moore out of the sand and walked him to a waiting police car. He knew he had panicked when he came out of the men's room and probably blew whatever plan Ethan had going. He was mad at himself.

Logan followed Ethan up the beach, pushing past reporters asking him questions. Ethan turned to the closest reporter. "We will have a statement soon." Then he and Logan climbed into their truck and pulled out of the parking lot.

Ethan looked over at Logan, "You okay? Do you need to get checked out?"

"I'm fine." Logan reassured him.

They drove in silence back to the office to do the paperwork and debrief and turn Moore over for extradition.

Ethan went into the office while the other team members unloaded the trucks and made sure they secured the prisoner in a holding cell. Logan was still fuming from the earlier events, and now he was wet on top of it all.

He strode over to where Jared was grabbing his go bag from the back of the truck. Logan grabbed him by the shoulder and slammed him against the side of the suburban.

"What the hell, man?" Jared roared.

"Boss keeps telling me I should lay off of you, but after that stunt tonight, I'm thinking you need your ass kicked."

"What stunt?"

"Coming out of the bathroom and panicking, you could have gotten people killed!"

"Screw you." Jared tried to push past Logan.

That was all Logan needed to hear. He slammed his enormous fist into Jared's face and let him sink to the ground.

Stephanie stepped outside in time to see Jared getting off the ground and taking a swing at Logan, just before the two of them locked arms and went down on the ground.

"Ethan!" She yelled as loud as she could. "Stop it you two," she grabbed at an arm she didn't know whose it was, it didn't matter they threw her off and continued fighting.

Ethan ran out and grabbed each one by the collar of their shirts. "Stop it right now or you'll have me to deal with!" He bellowed. Logan and Jared broke apart enough that Ethan stepped in between them. He shoved Logan hard backwards. "I said stop!"

He pushed Jared back and pointed to Stephanie, "Can you handle him?"

"Yeah, boss I got him." Stephanie grabbed Jared by the arm and marched him in the opposite direction of the office and Logan.

"Let me guess, you started it." Ethan turned on Logan.

Logan just stared at Ethan; he wasn't ready to talk. He was still angry.

"Okay," Ethan ran his hand through his hair in exasperation.

Logan breathed deeply, trying to regain control, "You saw what happened. He wasn't taking this seriously and he could have gotten one of us or a civilian injured today!"

"I know that and I," Ethan point at his own chest, "Will deal with Jared."

"You're right, I'm sorry I wasn't questioning you."

"I know you weren't, buddy. But you've been edgy lately and I think you've always had a thing against Jared and you better hope he doesn't press charges."

Logan leaned back against the suburban and shook his head. He hadn't lost control of his temper like that in a long time.

"Take a few days off, and that is not an option. Let me see if I can do a little damage control here."

"I'm sorry, Ethan."

"Don't apologize to me, apologize to Jared."

"I'm not ready to do that just yet."

Ethan shook his head in dismay at his friend. He'd never seen Logan this intense before. If it was over the girl Logan had mentioned, Logan in love was a dangerous thing.

"Logan, stay local, in case I need you, understand?"

Logan nodded and headed for his own truck and drove home. He was so keyed up he showered, changed clothes, then went for a run. After five miles he had worked out his frustration and his thoughts turned to Blake. He would call her tomorrow after he had some sleep and was hopefully closer to normal. He stopped running and put his hands on his hips for a minute and pictured Blake in his mind. Emotions warred within him; he could picture them at breakfast talking. The way her eyes would change to a deeper green. He thought about his job and the long hours and what that does to relationships. And then there was having to be accountable to someone else. Was it worth it? Part of him said 'yes'.

He walked back home and showered again. He ordered a pizza and fell asleep while watching old western movies.

CHAPTER EIGHT

With Logan out of the building, Ethan went in search of Jared. Stephanie was still with him and he was putting some ice on his eye. Logan had nailed him hard twice from the looks of it.

"Okay let's have it." Ethan said closing the door behind Stephanie as she left them to talk.

"I screwed up on this stakeout, Ethan. I shouldn't have gone up to the bathroom on the pier. I knew it was a risk, or at least I should have known that I could run into Moore. Logan was right, I could have blown the whole thing. It is only because of Logan we have the guy in custody."

Whatever Ethan was expecting, Jared to say in his own defense, this wasn't it. It took the wind out of his sails now that he didn't have to deliver the speech he had prepared in his head.

"Okay," Ethan nodded. "And what about the fight?"

"Well, I think Logan was a little rough on me, but I probably deserved it."

"Do you want to press charges?"

"What? Against Logan? No way, boss. In fact, if he still here I need to apologize to him; to all of you."

"No, I sent him home for a few days to cool off. Best let that alone for a while."

Jared nodded, "Sure, boss. But if you talk to him, can you tell him I'm sorry and I don't blame him?"

"Fine. But I'll tell you like I'll tell him. If this," Ethan pointed to Jared's face. "happens again, you both will suffer disciplinary action."

"Yes, sir."

"Now, go home. You're no good to me tonight."

Jared walked out the door like a scolded puppy. Ethan walked back to the office. Stephanie was at her desk working on the reports for the fugitive capture.

"Well, I sent the two of them home, so I guess it's just me and you." Ethan said.

Stephanie looked up and shook her head. "I don't know what's up with them."

"Hard to say, those two picks at each other constantly." Ethan not wanting to discuss the details.

"Well, I don't condone Logan's methods, but he wasn't wrong, Jared screwed up."

Ethan looked at her curiously. "Am I missing something?" Now he was wondering if there was more to this than just Logan being pissed off; and Jared for making a rookie mistake.

Stephanie looked down at her hands for a moment. She looked up at Ethan, "It has been nothing serious until now. Tonight, could have gone badly. For a minute when Moore grabbed that kid....," her voice trailed off.

Ethan sat down at his desk with a thud and faced Stephanie. "Start talking."

"Well, it isn't like he thumbs his nose at the rules or anything. I think he isn't as mature as he needs to be."

"So, he doesn't take the job seriously?"

"He understands its important, I think he just doesn't appreciate that we are not invincible. I think that is the part he hasn't realized yet."

Ethan listened carefully before speaking.

"Do you ever feel unsafe when you're out in the field with him?"

"No, but I'm pretty confident in my own abilities and I'm confident that ultimately Jared will do the right thing, I just think sometimes he takes unnecessary risks."

"I see." Ethan leaned forward in his chair, "I wish you had told me this sooner, today could have been prevented."

"You're absolutely right, and I regret it. I've been trying to guide him, and I didn't want him to get into trouble, he's my partner."

Ethan nodded, he understood her situation, but it was trending to an unsafe environment.

"Sounds like I need to make some changes to the team."

"Boss...,"

"Don't worry, no one is in trouble. But we need to make sure all of our teammates have what they need to be successful, and apparently I have failed Jared in that regard." He paused for a moment, "Is there anything else we should talk about?"

"No,"

"Are you comfortable talking to me?"

"Yes, I know I can talk to you about anything."

"Except about Jared,"

"Okay, but that was the only thing, and it won't happen again."

"I hope not. Go home, we'll finish this up in the morning."

"But...,"

"Go."

Clearly his team needed a break, and he needed to think. How had he missed the whole Jared thing? Logan had been telling him all along, and he wasn't listening. Today was as much his fault as Jared's, if not more.

***

Logan woke to the sound of his cell phone chirping. He was still in the chair; an infomercial was on the TV and the half-eaten pizza lay in the box on the coffee table.

He sat up, the muscles in his neck and shoulders protesting. He checked the phone a text from Ethan had come in.

"No charges, will call later."

Logan tossed the phone back onto the table and stood up. He needed coffee and a hot shower. Once he felt human again, he picked up the phone and called Blake.

"Hello?"

"Hi, it's Logan."

Her voice changed, and she sounded more relaxed. "Hi,"

"Listen, I have a couple of days off I wasn't expecting, I was wondering what your schedule was and if you'd like to...," He suddenly was panic-stricken, what if she said no, "spend some time together?"

"I have to work today, but then I'm off for the next two days. Did you have anything in mind?"

"Well, I thought you'd still like to have those fishing lessons, or take a drive somewhere; the eastern shore or something?"

"Yeah, that sounds great. Are you okay?"

Her question surprised Logan.

"Sure, why?"

"You don't strike me as the type of guy who randomly takes a couple of days off from work."

He laughed a little, "Well, I'm trying something new."

Blake laughed too, Logan thought it was the first time he had heard her laugh, and he liked the way it sounded.

"Okay, then it is a semi plan." Logan said, relieved that she had agreed to see him again.

"I get off work at seven tonight, do you want to have a late dinner or something?"

She surprised him for the second time; he liked she could surprise him. "Yeah, that would be great. I'll drop by the store."

"Okay, see you later."

"See you later." Logan clicked off and stared at the phone. He was excited and suddenly terrified. What was he thinking? He started breathing heavy. What was happening? Why did he think this was even remotely a good idea? He didn't like not being in control of his emotions, and he seemed to lose control of them more and more lately. If his is what love did to you, then perhaps he didn't need it after all.

He felt like a caged animal, there was no way he could stay in the house until time to meet Blake tonight. He looked down at his phone; he needed help. After last night he didn't think talking to Ethan about it was a good idea and that only left one person he could call.

He reluctantly punched in the number and waited.

"Hello,"

"Hey, it's Logan."

"How are you doing, Logan?"

"Not so good, listen I really hate to bother you, but I'm desperate. Can we talk, privately?" There was a slight pause, and he held his breath, waiting for the rejection.

"Sure, where?"

"Your place?

"Yes, let me move some things around can you be here in an hour?"

"Listen, if it is too much trouble,"

"Don't be ridiculous, I expect to see you at one, don't be late."

Silence filled his ear. She had hung up. Logan sighed, he drove downtown and found a place to park his truck amid all the small electric cars and sub-compacts in the underground parking garage.

He took the elevator to the top floor. The receptionist greeted him, "Can I help you, sir?"

"My name is Logan Watson; I have an appointment."

"Just a moment."

He couldn't bring himself to sit down. Offices like this made him nervous and fidgety. He stood staring at the large, framed photos and artwork on the wall. He had the urge to pace, but the arrangement of chairs and the oversized coffee table made it impossible.

The large wooden door to the left of the reception desk opened.

"Logan, come on in."

He did as he was told, not making eye contact with the receptionist as he walked by.

The door closed behind him.

"Logan, are you okay? You look like hell."

Logan stared down at Kay Dandridge. The woman Ethan had yearned for, for over six years. He studied Kay's face, "Kay, I need your help. Did he tell you about it?"

"He told me you punched Jared out last night."

"Yeah, I did. I don't know why; I mean, he's young, he just needs to learn."

"But you're not here because of Jared. You and Ethan can work that out."

"You're right. I wish it were that easy."

"I am curious why you are here." Kay returned to her chair behind the desk.

"I'm here because of Blake."

Kay smiled and leaned back in her chair.

"Whose Blake?"

"She works at Bumboat Books and she is the most perfect and beautiful woman I've ever met, and I am all twisted up inside over her and I don't understand why."

Kay watched Logan's face change, so many emotions. She repressed the urge to smile.

"Can, I get you anything? Water, coffee, something stronger?"

Logan's train of thought changed, "You have something stronger in your office? Does Ethan know that?"

"Ethan doesn't have to know everything, and besides, there are perks to owning your own company. The rules are what I say they are." She laughed as she got up and poured him a bourbon.

"Do these rules apply to your employees as well?"

"No, they don't own the company."

They shared a laugh, and Logan downed the bourbon.

"Better?" Kay asked, reaching for the empty glass.

"Yes, thank you."

She put the glass on the corner of her desk and set down in the guest chair next to Logan.

"Now, why don't you tell me all about Blake."

"That's the crazy thing, I can't. I know nothing about her. She is beautiful. She has the most amazing eyes. She is shy but also not."

"What else do you know?"

"She moved here because she had a nasty breakup, a divorce. The details are not clear. I know it was bad enough that she left her hometown to get away from whoever it was. She's hard to get to know, she isn't forthcoming with information, but she can read me like a book." He shook his head, smiling.

Kay watched Logan as he spoke. It was clear he was in love with this woman, and it was also clear he was fighting it.

"Logan, what are you so afraid of?" She asked when he finally stopped talking.

"I'm not sure I like the way I feel right now."

"You don't enjoy being in love?"

"Not if this is what it is like."

"What you are describing is your fear of not being in control. All I can tell you is that you have to accept it because if you are truly in love with Blake, that will not change. Look at Ethan and I."

"That is why I came to you. You guys fell in love right away, and it was six years before you met each other again. Did you feel like this the whole six year?"

"Yes. And that begs the question have you tried talking to Ethan about all of this?"

"Yes, and no. I mean, he basically just keeps telling me that this is how it is, and I need to suck it up."

Kay laughed. "He is not always very helpful when giving advice on what to do with your emotions."

"No, he isn't."

Kay sighed, "Look, Ethan and I were a mess for a long time. And we all handle it differently. Logan, you have options that were not open to us. It doesn't have to be like it was for you and Blake."

Logan sighed, "I thought love was supposed to be this magic thing that made your life worth living. But after watching you and Ethan and now this, I don't know." He shook his head, dismayed.

"Ethan and I didn't have a choice. I was working overseas for a while; Ethan was married to Diane, things were complicated. I also refused to be a party to a broken marriage, so I stayed away, but my love for him, never went away. I knew I would never be in love with anyone else."

"What would you have done, if you two hadn't found each other again?"

"I don't know. I probably would have died a miserable old spinster."

Logan shook his head.

"Blake is right here, right now, and not married. You have no reason not to pursue this relationship and be happy."

"But what if she loves me as much as I love her, and then what?"

"Then you live your life blissfully happy?"

Logan frowned at Kay.

"Okay, so what you're afraid of commitment? Of losing your freedom?"

"Possibly?"

"Has Ethan turned into some sort of homebody since we have been together?"

"No,"

"Logan, you are one of the bravest, most bad-ass people I have ever met. You saved Ethan's life in a gun battle last year, and I can't believe you're afraid of this."

"I'm afraid of things I can't see and control."

"Well, buddy, you're going to have to suck it up, life is full of things you can't control." Kay chuckled. "When are you going to see Blake again?"

"Tonight, we are going to have dinner and tomorrow we're going fishing."

"Well, that is perfect, because fishing with you isn't easy and if she can handle that, then she can handle anything, including you."

"What do you mean, fishing with me isn't easy?"

"Do you remember the first time you and I fished together? It was on the bay with Jared and his friend, you gave me such a hard time."

"I don't remember it quite like that." Logan looked away because he did remember giving Kay a hard time and Kay could give as good as she got, and she showed him up with her fishing skills.

There were voices in the outer office. Kay could hear her personal assistant, Sherry's voice.

"Ethan, Kay is with someone and I don't think she wants to be disturbed right now."

"Really? Who?"

Sherry was silent for a moment.

"A..., Logan Watson."

"Logan, really?"

There was a brief knock, and the door opened. Logan felt his heart sink.

Ethan walked in and looked from Kay to Logan.

"So last night you punch out a fellow agent and today you're chatting up my girl? You do like to live, dangerously don't you?"

Logan stood up and faced Ethan. Kay watched with an amused look.

"I don't consider it dangerous."

"No? And why is that?"

"Last night was a punk ass kid, and today it is an old man."

Ethan stared Logan down for a moment, then they both started laughing. They pounded each other on the back.

Kay deftly swept the glass off of the corner of her desk and took it over to sit in the sink next to the coffeemaker to wash later.

"Seriously, what are you doing here?" Ethan looked at Logan, concerned.

"Just getting a fresh perspective on things. Listen, I'd better go." He looked over at Kay. "Thank you."

Kay walked over and stood on her toes to hug Logan. He bent down and kissed her cheek.

"Take care of yourself." She whispered in his ear. He nodded.

He extended his hand to Ethan, "See ya later,"

"Monday. I expect to see you Monday morning."

Logan looked at him questioningly, but only nodded. "See you then."

After Logan left, Ethan bent down to kiss her. "So, what did Logan have to say?"

"He is a mess, Ethan. I imagine a lot like you might have been at one time. He's scared about his feelings for this girl Blake and what that might mean. He doesn't feel in control and that is a problem for him."

Ethan nodded, "I thought it might be something along those lines." He reached out and took her hand affectionately, "Are you going to offer me whatever Logan was drinking?"

Kay looked at him in surprise.

"Don't worry, you did a good job whisking that glass off the desk. Most people probably wouldn't have noticed." He grinned and hugged her.

"Sometimes being with an FBI agent has its disadvantages." She laughed and poured him a cup of coffee.

"This is not what Logan was drinking,"

"No, but Logan wasn't on duty either." She swatted at him and sat down behind her desk. "So, what's on your mind?"

CHAPTER NINE

Logan survived the day without losing his mind until time for Blake to get off work. He stood outside the bookstore, waiting patiently.

"Hi," Blake said breathlessly as she looked at Logan in his dress slacks and collared shirt.

"Hi," He smiled. "Any preferences?"

"Not really,"

"Okay, what about food allergies, likes, dislikes?"

Blake laughed a little, "No allergies that I know of, I don't like anchovies."

"Okay, well, let's avoid seafood since we are fishing tomorrow. But about, Italian? There's a great place just up the street."

"Sounds perfect."

They walked casually, two blocks to Momma Rosa's. Blake saw the heads turn as they walked in. They were seated in a booth and she giggled at Logan, trying to squeeze into it. She got settled and then discreetly pulled the table towards her.

He looked at her as if it embarrassed him.

"I'm sorry, you didn't mind that I did that, did you? It's just that the table was so far away."

He smiled knowing that she was lying, and that she had done it for him, but he loved her for doing it and for not allowing him to feel uncomfortable about it.

"Thank you," he whispered. She smiled and waived him off. Afterall, when you're tall, muscular and built like he was, she imagined it was difficult for him to squeeze into a lot of places normal people could fit into.

A smiling server appeared with two glasses of water and menus.

"I'll be right back," She said as she headed to the next table.

"Do you come here often?"

"Not really, I mean I have their pizza delivered, but I don't dine-in."

"Why not?"

"Too many late nights at work, I guess. Never really had a reason to."

Blake smiled. She understood he didn't date much. That was good, at least he wasn't a player.

The server returned, "Ready to order?"

Logan raised his eyebrows at Blake as if to ask if she was ready.

"Do you want to share a calzone?"

Logan smiled, "Yeah, that sounds great."

The server looked like she was impatient, "What would you like in it?"

She nodded, "How about Pepperoni, sausage and black olives?"

Logan smiled like Christmas had come early. "And two beers."

"You got it," The server took the menus and rushed off to the next customer.

"Blake Morgan, you are full of surprises." He grinned at her.

"Oh, yeah, I am a woman of mystery." She laughed out loud. Logan laughed with her.

"You said you were working on a case recently, is it anything you can talk about? Or want to talk about?"

"Yeah, it isn't secret or anything. There was a guy that killed his family in another state several years ago and he has been seen here recently. We tracked him down and arrested him."

"Wow, that is amazing, so those cold cases really get solved."

"Sometimes. It can take a while, but as the technology improves; we can retest things we couldn't test before. Or a lead pans out. Someone recognized the suspect and called us."

"That is fascinating. Do you do any of that?"

"No, I'm strictly a field agent, I do a lot of research on the computer, and then execute the warrants when we have them."

"Isn't that dangerous?"

"Yeah, it can be." He tried to downplay it.

"This is a lame question; have you ever been shot in the line of duty?"

"Not while working for the FBI, but my boss, Ethan, got shot last year during a warehouse raid."

"Wow, that is scary. Is he okay now?"

"Oh yeah, he was wearing his vest, so he was fine."

"I'm glad to hear it. I'm also glad it wasn't you." She whispered.

He smiled at her as the calzone, and beer arrived.

They ate, drank beer, and Blake told him about all the unique characters that came into the bookstore and the stories she made up to fill in the gaps of what she knew about their lives. Like how Ms. Goldstein, who was always reading true crime, was actually an amateur detective looking for clues in her next case.

Logan laughed the animated way she described each character.

They paid their bill and left; Logan offered to drive her home.

"You don't have to do that. You've been drinking I can't in good conscious let you drive."

"Yes, but I'm bigger than you and ate more so my body has absorbed more alcohol than you."

"Well, can't argue with that logic."

"Good, where do you live?"

She gave him the address. As they pulled into her apartment complex a car rushed out, nearly hitting them.

"Whoa!" Logan slammed on the brakes.

Blake barely got a glimpse of the driver or the car, but something in the back of her mind said it was Jerry. But that didn't even make sense. How could he have found her apartment? She had changed her name and her profession. She decided it was the beer, and she was imagining things.

Logan walked her to her apartment.

"Thank you." She said after unlocking the door.

"Thank you, I had a great time. Still want to go fishing in the morning?"

"Of course."

"Great, I'll pick up you here at eight, that will give us enough time to get out to the cottage and get set up on the pier before the tide comes in."

She nodded, nervous and excited about agreeing to go to his river cottage and fish. Isn't this how horror movies started? She inhaled, "See you in the morning."

She turned and disappeared inside and slowly closed the door.

Logan waited to hear the lock click over before leaving.

He felt like he was floating on air.

***

The next morning, Logan was at Blake's apartment promptly at eight. He knocked softly on the door. A few minutes passed, and he wondered if she had overslept or reconsidered. He waited a few more minutes and knocked again, a little harder this time.

The door popped open, "Hey, good morning."

Logan stood marveling at how good she looked in jeans and an oversized sweatshirt with her hair in a ponytail. "You ready to catch some fish?"

"Absolutely!" She beamed.

"Alright, let's go."

Pulling out of the parking lot, Blake noticed the car from the previous night sitting across the street. Blake strained to see the driver fearing it might be Jerry.

Logan noticed her interest in the car, "Everything alright?"

"Yeah, I was just thinking that was the car that almost hit us last night." She tried to sound casual.

Logan looked in his side mirror and made a mental note of the license plate number. Then watched to see if the car tried to follow them. But it didn't move. He watched Blake out of the corner of his eye. She seemed nervous, like she was trying to check the mirror without him noticing.

After about thirty minutes they were out of the populated area and fewer cars were on the road, as the landscape changed Blake relaxed.

"This is beautiful out here," she pressed the button to lower the window. "Wow, you can really smell the salt air."

"Almost there," Logan turned onto the dirt road that led to his weekend cottage on the water.

Blake looked around it the cottage wasn't isolated and not at all scary. It was open and while it was private, she could see other cottages. She felt silly for her worries the night before and images of horror movies in remote places.

Logan watched her as she stretched and looked around. "Not exactly serial killer territory, is it?" He laughed.

She blushed and looked embarrassed. "How did you guess?"

"If someone invited me to a weekend cottage to go fishing, that would be the first thing I would think of." He laughed some more. "Don't worry, you're safe with me and if at any moment you want to leave or are uncomfortable, you just let me know. In fact, here is my bosses' card. Call him at any point if you think I am a threat, and he will come and shoot me and rescue you."

She laughed and looked at the card as she tried to hand it back.

"No, keep it." Logan insisted, "Want to go inside?"

Blake was surprised to find how open and airy the cottage was. It had a tasteful nautical décor, none of that old fish net on the wall stuff. "This is beautiful."

"Thank you. Let me show you around a little," He led her to the kitchen, "help yourself to the fridge, bathrooms and bedrooms are down that hallway."

She nodded. He was such a gentleman but not in the overt way that Jerry and been, no there was enough bad boy lurking just below the surface of Logan to make her appreciate his gentlemanly efforts. If she was honest, she wouldn't mind seeing a little more of that hidden bad boy.

"You want coffee or anything, or you ready to fish?"

"I'm ready to fish!"

Logan smiled this would be better than fishing with Kay. "Okay," He showed her the way out the back door past his outdoor kitchen and onto the pier.

"First you want to get familiar with the rod and reel and how things work." He showed her how to hold the rod, how to bait the hook with live bait, and how to cast out into the river. Once she settled in, he tossed his line into the water and they stood quietly side by side. Blake taking in the surroundings and Logan admiring her profile in the sun.

Finally, her pole dipped, and she had a fish.

"Pull it up quick like I showed you now start reeling it in." He left his pole and stepped behind her to help. "That's it, you got it!"

"Is that a big one, it looks big."

"Yes, it is big enough to eat, you want to keep it and cook it up later?"

She grinned and nodded, "Yeah, lets catch some more."

Logan laughed and checked his line, nothing yet.

Blake cast out again and waited. She was having a great time, and she tried not to think about how hard his body was against hers. That his arms were as hard as steel ropes and when he put them around her, they were a complete distraction. His muscles were from something more than the gym.

"How long were you in the military?" She wondered about the fitness requirements for the military and the FBI.

"Six years in the Army, most of it overseas."

"Oh, that sounds dangerous,"

"It was,"

She changed the subject, "Do you come here every weekend?"

"If I'm not working, yeah. It is a place to disconnect from everything and just relax. Its important I think to take some time for yourself."

His comment surprised her, but it made her happy. Could he be for real?

"Do you share this place with friends often?" She wondered how many girls he had brought here.

"Uh, not really. Ethan, my boss, is the only other person who has ever been out here. Well, Ethan and Kay."

"Wow!" She looked back towards the house it was a great setup for entertaining, yet he seemed to be a man who liked his privacy. "I can understand, it is so beautiful and quiet without having to travel too far. It is perfect."

"Yeah, it is convenient. I'm glad you like it, though." He smiled at her just as his line got a hit, and she watched as the muscles in his arms worked as he reeled in a fish.

"He held it up for her, another keeper," He smiled, "dinner for sure tonight."

She laughed. She thought how she could get used to living in a place like this.

"Do you like Gates Point? Do you think you might stay around?" He asked, trying to sound casual.

"Yeah, I only signed a six-month lease on the apartment to give me time to get the lay of the land before I do anything long term." She looked over at him, "I have to admit starting out on my own is pretty scary and not knowing anyone here has been a little tougher than I thought."

"I think its pretty brave to leave everything familiar and come to a new place you've only ever seen in a magazine. I'm not sure I could do that." He admired her.

She waved him off, "Oh please, I'm not brave. Not like you, being a soldier and an agent. Getting shot at all the time. All I did was tuck tail and run."

He frowned, "Don't sell yourself short, bravery comes in many forms."

"I suppose."

"Do you mind if I ask why you left it all behind and came here?"

"I married my college sweetheart. He was charming and all of that, and he had a good job as an accountant. I thought it was 'safe', some sort of storybook life. But he changed, I'm not sure when. I don't know how or why, but it got to where he was angry all the time. And I couldn't understand it, we had everything, a beautiful house, solid careers, members of all the right socials clubs, but he started drinking and became controlling." She paused and looked over at him. "Long story short, we got into an argument one night over nothing, really nothing, and he hit me." She noticed the muscles in Logan's shoulders tighten. "It was one time, but that is all it took. I would not wait around for an apology or fool myself into believing he was still a good man. I stayed long enough to get the divorced finalized, and then I left. I changed my last name, and I came here, I guess I wanted a fresh start; to figure out who I really am, without a husband."

Logan nodded, her story wasn't unfamiliar, but he had been right about her before she was brave, and she had a good head on her shoulders. He wished more abused spouses could do what she did. He also knew he had to be careful not to crowd her. She was trying to find herself, and he needed to let her do that. He hoped her new life included him, but he would not force her into anything. Even though every fiber of his being was screaming for her.

"Like I said before, you are very brave." He caught another fish. "Want something to drink?" He offered.

"Sure."

"Water, iced tea, soda?"

"Iced tea would be wonderful. Need any help."

"No, you stay here and relax, I'll be right back."

Blake removed her shoes and sat down to let her feet dangle into the water. She was used to the ice-cold water that ran down from the mountain tops; this was a little warmer. But still it wasn't anything you wanted to swim in even at this temperature.

Logan returned with their drinks. He pulled their lines in. "Here you go."

"Thank you,"

"Do any of the other cottages along the river ever come on the market?"

"I'm sure they do from time to time. You want to move out here?"

"It is so beautiful and quiet."

Just then a boat zipped up the river heading to the marina. Logan tracked it until it was out of site. "It is quiet most of the time. It's also a long commute every day. Speaking of work," He changed the subject, "What kind of workload will you have with the college?"

"The first semester I'll be teaching two classes so nothing too heavy and only undergraduates. I only have a master's degree, so I can't teach graduate level courses, but that is okay."

"Would you want to get your Ph.D.?"

"I don't know, I mean, never say never, right? But it isn't anything I've ever thought about." She looked away for a moment, and Logan thought he could see that she still felt the pain of her past life. "I thought I'd always be working in a firm; Perhaps even have my own firm one day."

"Why don't you? I'm sure there are several firms that would be happy to have you here."

"Yeah, I just thought that it would be safer to try a different profession for a while?"

"Safer?"

"I'm probably being paranoid, but I thought if Jerry, that's my ex, ever wanted to find me he'd start with architectural firms and I thought I should," She paused not liking the way the words sounded in her own ears. "Try not to make it so easy for him to find me."

"If you hide from him, he still wins." Logan whispered. "It's smart to be safe, but you shouldn't live in fear. If you are only teaching because you think it is a safe place to hide; first, your wrong because if he wants to find you, he will no matter what you do, second, it isn't fair to you or the students if your heart isn't in it."

Blake looked away. He had a point, and she was ashamed of herself now for hiding. She found she couldn't look him in the eye; she felt like a coward. "You're right." She choked out.

"Hey," He reached out and touched her arm. "I'm not judging, you do what you need to do. Teach for a semester see how you like it. You might like it better than being in a big firm."

"Do you really believe that?"

"I believe things happen for a reason and that you won't know until you try."

She smiled at him, "Thank you."

"Well, the fish will stop biting soon. Have you ever been kayaking?"

"No, I haven't."

"Can you swim?"

"Yes."

"Then I can teach you the rest, come on."

Logan stood up and walked up the pier. Blake followed, noticing a couple of kayaks on a rack near the back of the house. They were sleek, and she wondered what in the world she was thinking. Logan took one down and set it on the ground.

"They look unstable, but they really aren't you just have to understand how it moves and that if it wobbles doesn't mean you're going to fall in. The worst thing you can do is panic, okay?"

She nodded. He knelt down at the bow. "I'm going to roll it back and forth while you get in so you get a feel for what it will be like on the water." He nodded to her. She looked at him dubiously but followed his instruction. He gently rocked the kayak while she stepped inside, crouching down to steady herself, then sat all the way down.

"See, that wasn't so bad." Logan smiled at her.

"No, that wasn't too hard."

"Think you want to try it out there?"

"Why not?" She said her heart racing, as disastrous possibilities ran through her mind. Logan must have read the look on her face because he chuckled.

"I promise not to let anything happen to you, trust me?"

"Yes,"

"Okay." He nodded, "Here is a life jacket, keep it on at all times, there is a whistle attached right here, if you think I am too far away, and you get into trouble blow on this."

She nodded.

"Here is your paddle, don't worry if you drop it, it will float with these." He pointed to two inflatable squares. "Questions?"

"Just one, will this thing sink?"

"Only if it gets too much water inside of it and that is not likely to happen, but if it does," he laughed, "Don't worry about it, that one is Ethan's."

"Oh great, that is all I need is to have you get in trouble at work because I sunk your bosses' kayak."

Logan shook his head, "It will be fine, it won't sink, and he hasn't used it in a long time, he won't be that upset about it."

After a couple more minutes, they were ready to go. "You still okay with this?" Logan asked one last time.

"I'll be fine." She nodded.

"Okay," he drug her kayak and put part of it in the water. "Get in and then I will push you out, don't paddle, just float."

She nodded. Her heart pounded as she stepped into the kayak. Logan slid the paddle in alongside her. "It's okay to hold on to the sides."

Then he pushed her into the water, then slid his kayak in, waded into the water and deftly climbed aboard. He paddled up next to her.

"Okay, so far?"

She smiled widely. "Yeah, this is cool."

He nodded, "Okay, grab your paddle and do one side and then the other, all the way into the water." He showed her the technique. She pulled ahead of him as she tried the paddle. The kayak wobbled, and she stopped.

Logan paddled two strokes and was up next to her. "Put, your knees up against the sides where those pads are, that will help keep it stable."

She looked over at his kayak and mimicked him.

"Now just take it slow, we aren't in any hurry."

She nodded and relaxed a little; he paddled lightly so she could easily keep up with him.

The river widened, and the current was a little stronger.

"Logan?" She said, getting a little nervous.

"You're okay, just stay close to the shoreline. I'm right here."

She glanced over at him. Her neck was stiff, and she realized how tense she was.

Logan came alongside and reached over to grab her Kayak. "It's okay, Blake, I will keep you safe. But I do want to show you something, okay?"

She smiled tightly and nodded.

"We are going to move away from the shore out that way," he pointed to the open water, "not far".

"What about the waves?"

"We aren't going that close to the waves."

"Alright then."

"Do what I do,"

She nodded and watched how he paddled and leaned just as the kayak turned away from shore. The ripples on the water got slightly bigger, nothing you could really call a wave, but it was exciting. She felt like she was on a kiddie roller coaster at the county fair back home. She smiled, then laughed as they bobbed up and down. Logan looked over and smiled. It was good to see her laughing and enjoying herself on the water. They started paralleling the shoreline, and it didn't take long before it happened. A dolphin came up alongside of her kayak.

"Uh, Logan!" Blake tried holding up her paddle above the kayak.

"It's okay, Blake, It's okay. Don't paddle, just wait for it." The rest of the pod joined them and starting swimming alongside.

"Okay, paddle some more,"

She looked over at Logan and again copied his movements; the dolphins followed along for a while then swam ahead to go play in the waves.

Logan paddled over to her, "What did you think?"

"That was amazing!"

He studied her face. She had a glow about her, and Logan hoped that there would be a day when she always had that glow and not the fear and worry that creased her forehead more than it should.

"Here," he handed her a bottle of water.

"Thank you," She hadn't realized how thirsty she was. She watched the dolphins playing while she drank.

"They are so beautiful," not realizing she said it out loud.

"I agree," Logan whispered.

"Wanna head back and cook our fish?"

She looked longingly at the waves and dolphins she wanted this moment to last forever. "Okay."

Logan paddled up to the shore next to his pier and hopped out, then waded back into the water to pull Blake ashore.

"You don't have to do that," she protested.

"I don't want you to get wet."

"I think I'm already wet."

"Indulge me."

He scooped her up and carried her to the grass.

"Whoa!" She cried, not expecting to be lifted and carried ashore in Logan's arms.

Logan grabbed both kayaks at the bow and drug them completely out of the water.

"That was impressive."

"I love going out and having a pod swim along,"

"I meant you, but yes, that was impressive too. I think that is the closest thing to a religious experience I've ever had."

Logan smiled, he understood how she felt. It had been the same for him the first time a pod joined him.

"Here, drink some more water," Logan handed her another bottle. He smiled and left no room for argument. "It's easy to get dehydrated even when it is chilly out."

Blake took the bottle, "What can I do to help?"

"Stand there and look supportive." He instructed.

She laughed. "I'm not sure what that looks like."

Blake walked over and picked up the paddles and carried them to their home at the rack. She took off the life vest and handed it to Logan.

With all the gear stored, they headed into the cottage.

"If you'd like to freshen up, the bathroom is just down there on the left."

"Thanks."

Blake returned to the kitchen to find Logan with a towel over his shoulder and cleaning the fish.

"Anything I can do?"

"You any good at chopping vegetables?"

"I've chopped one or two in my life."

He grinned at her. He gave her a cutting board, knife and skewers for the grill.

"Okay, let's see what you can do."

"Game on!" She took the knife and began chopping the vegetables into cubes. When she finished, she looked over at Logan.

"Okay, what's next?"

He made a show of inspecting her work, "How are you with salad?"

"Fair," she gave him a steely gaze.

"Hmm, okay, I'll give you a shot, rookie."

He produced a large salad bowl from the top shelf in the cabinet and provided her with more vegetables. He left her to it while he took the fish outside to the grill.

She helped set the table inside.

"Do you prefer beer or wine?" Logan asked.

"Whatever you are having is fine with me."

"I think wine, tonight." He grinned.

They ate and drank and talked about living in the mountains versus living along the water. And they laughed as she explained the term 'flatlander' to him.

After dinner they returned to the deck and Logan turned on the outdoor heater. The sun was setting and cast its long shadows over the deck. Blake was feeling the effects of the wine and her eyelids were getting droopy. She and Logan sat watching the stars slowly appear. Logan's heart swelled in his chest as her head rested on his upper arm. Blake fell asleep. He knew he should take her home, but he couldn't bear the thought of how quiet the cottage would be without her in it. He had enjoyed their day together, and he didn't want it to end. Logan sat for a long while and listened to her breathing he felt very protective of her in a way that he had never felt before. it scared him at the same time it made him feel whole; like he now understood his purpose in life. It was to protect Blake. Finally, he carried her to his bedroom and laid her on the bed, he pulled a blanket cover her and returned to the deck to thank whatever gods were among those stars for bringing Blake to him.

CHAPTER TEN

Monday morning came too soon, Logan woke up with a new outlook, he still had to face Ethan and Jared. But after spending the weekend with Blake, he felt like he could face anything.

Ethan was already in the office when he arrived.

"Morning, Ethan."

Ethan looked up and cocked at eyebrow in Logan's direction.

"Morning, Logan. Did you have a pleasant weekend?"

"Yes, I did. In fact, I had a great weekend. How about you? You and Kay do anything fun?"

Ethan slowly rose from his chair and walked over to Logan was standing still holding his go bag. Ethan made a circle, looking Logan up and down.

"Uh Ethan, you want to tell me what you are doing?"

"You look different, you sound different, and you are acting differently, and I am trying to figure out why."

"Same old me."

"I don't think so. Did you drink this weekend?"

"Just a beer or two and a wine with dinner Saturday night."

"Wine, you say?" Ethan studied him further.

"Yeah, white wine with fish, surely Kay has introduced you to wine by now."

"Yes, yes. I have had wine from time to time."

"So, what's the big deal?"

"The big deal is that you are normally hung over on Monday mornings. You are grumpy before you've had at least three cups of coffee and you're not even carrying a cup with you, so I am concerned."

"I left my coffee on the counter at home. I promise to go pour another cup if you stop staring at me."

"Go ahead," Ethan made a grand sweeping motion to the kitchen, while suppressing a grin. Kay had told him that Logan had planned to see Blake this weekend, and it was obvious from Logan's mood things had gone well.

Logan put his bag down behind his desk and headed for the kitchen. He would not let Ethan get the better of him, and he would not tell Ethan anything either. He would let Ethan guess if he wanted to.

By the time he returned to the bullpen, Stephanie and Jared were walking in. Jared was still sporting some bruises and Logan winced at the memory of his behavior.

"Okay, now that Logan has had his coffee, and everyone is here, we are going to have a staff meeting."

Everyone looked at Ethan, stunned; they had never had a staff meeting before.

Jared looked at the floor, "this is because of me isn't it?"

"No," Ethan said, "It is because of me. I have been negligent in training all of you, and I am going to fix that right now."

They all stood looking at him, waiting for whatever was coming next.

Logan took a step forward, "Wait, before you say anything more, I'd like to say something."

One side of Ethan's mouth twitched.

"Jared, I acted like a complete ass, last week and I shouldn't have. We've all made mistakes or had things go down differently than planned. I'm sorry I took it out on you." Logan offered his hand to Jared.

Jared looked at Logan, stunned for a moment, then shook his hand. "I'm sorry for screwing up, and I'm sure glad you were there to bail my ass out."

"Anytime."

Ethan cleared his throat, and everyone turned their attention back to him. "Good, now that is out of the way, Logan and Jared are now partners, Stephanie, you are with me."

Everyone looked at Ethan, not completely in agreement with this new arrangement.

"Jared, this will give you some insight into Logan's ability to see the big picture strategically. Logan, you will learn a fresh set of management skills, by mentoring Jared. Stephanie, you and I will focus on management and leadership skills. Tactically, your rolls will remain the same."

The team nodded and got back to work. Logan put his cell phone up on his desk where he could see it. He wasn't sure if Blake would text him. He had been relieved that she wasn't mad when she woke up in his bed the Sunday morning. He had stayed out on the deck most of the night thinking about Blake being so close yet so far away.

He had given her coffee and driven her home. They spoke on the phone Sunday night and she told him she had a wonderful time. She was opening the store today and would get off at six but hadn't committed to seeing him afterwards.

"Everything, alright?" Ethan asked him.

"What? Oh, yeah."

"Sure?"

"Yeah, I'm sure." Remembering the car that he and Blake had seen twice over the weekend, he picked up the desk phone and called a friend at the Gates Point Police department, "Hey Sean, it's Logan. Yeah, I need a favor running down a lead." Logan spoke casually, but as quietly as he could into the phone.

"Yeah, sure, what do you have?" Sgt. Sean Deavers asked.

Logan recited the number, "Just text me whatever you have."

"You got it."

Logan hung up.

"Got something?" Ethan asked.

"Not really, just playing a hunch."

***

"Hi, Blake. I'm here." Wendy called as she breezed through the front door.

"Oh hey," Blake poked her head over top of the magazine rack.

"How's business this morning?"

"It has been slow, one or two of the regulars have been in, but it is Monday, so it might pick up later." Blake said brightly.

"Sounds like you had a lovely weekend." Wendy smiled.

"I did, I had a date, sort of." Blake giggled.

Wendy stopped what she was doing "A date? With whom?"

Blake tried to pretend like it was no big deal, but she was bursting to tell someone. "Oh, it wasn't a date in a traditional sense, Logan took me fishing."

"Logan!" Wendy's mouth dropped open, "Girl, if I were twenty years younger, I'd be all over that one!"

"He is quite handsome." Blake tried to remain neutral.

"Handsome is an understatement. I could spread him on a cracker!"

Blake laughed out loud she couldn't keep it in any longer. "Right?"

"Come, tell me everything!" Wendy grabbed her wrist and pulled her to a couple of customer chairs near the magazine rack.

"He picked me up Saturday morning, and we drove out to his cottage he owns down along the river."

"He has a river cottage?"

"Yeah, and it is so beautiful there it has a pier, so we fished until we caught enough for dinner."

"And you weren't worried about being alone with him?"

"No, that's the thing, it is like he knew I was apprehensive, so he made sure I had my cell phone, he gave me his bosses' business card with an emergency number and said if I thought he acted inappropriately call that number that Ethan would get there faster than the police. He didn't crowd me at all. He was so thoughtful the entire weekend."

Wendy wasn't surprised, she had known Logan for a few years as a customer and then as a friend and knew in her heart Logan would never do anything to hurt Blake.

"We grilled the fish and had a wonderful dinner."

"What did you do between fishing and grilling?"

"We kayaked, and the best part, a pod of dolphins came up and swam with us, Wendy I'm telling you it was the most beautiful thing I have ever experienced."

Wendy smiled to herself. Seemed like Logan had really outdone himself.

"Then he brought me home on Sunday."

"Sunday! You spent the night with him?" Wendy was shocked.

"It wasn't like that at all. Neither of us wanted the night to end. I fell asleep sitting with him watching the stars and we both had wine with dinner, so he let me sleep in his room and he slept, on the deck, I think. At least that is where he was when I got up."

"Blake,"

"I was fully dressed; I still had my shoes on and everything." She laughed, "I didn't think you were a prude."

"I'm not, but still there are rules."

"Well, first we didn't kiss or hold hands or anything and second, I have a second chance at life, I think I'm going to say forget the rules for once! Look where they got me in the past."

Wendy took a serious tone, "That's all fine and good, but just because you want to live by a fresh set of rules doesn't mean there aren't still consequences, so be careful."

"What consequences?"

"To my knowledge, Logan has never had a serious relationship. When a guy Logan falls hard for a girl, I mean really falls in love. There isn't any going back. Just make sure you are ready to have a serious relationship again before you get too involved with Logan."

Blake looked at Wendy for a moment. She was blessed to have met two of the most caring people in the world. "I promise not to hurt Logan, and I appreciate you, too." Blake leaned over and hugged Wendy.

"Oh, well goodness, no point in getting teary-eyed at work," Wendy hopped up and looked around for a distraction, "Lots to do, lots to do."

Blake laughed, because there wasn't much to do. She had done it all before Wendy got there.

CHAPTER ELEVEN

Logan's phone buzzed with a message from Sean.

"Rental car. Rented three days ago at the airport, by a Mr. Jerry Townson." Logan's hand gripped the phone so hard his fingers ached. He sent a text back to Sean, "Thanks."

Conflicted about what he should do next, he walked into the kitchen. A moment later, Ethan followed him.

"Everything alright?"

"Yeah." Logan snapped.

Ethan began drifting about the kitchen to keep his movements calm and deliberate. He got two bottles of water out of the fridge and handed one to Logan, "Wanna, step outside for a minute? Get some fresh air?"

"Yeah, okay." Logan braced himself for what was coming.

"Bad news?"

"Not really."

"You were Mr. Happy Go Lucky this morning, then you did a one-eighty after receive a text, something is up with you man, and as a friend, I want you to understand you can talk to me. As your boss, you need to make sure your head is in this game, got it?"

Logan nodded, he wasn't ready to talk to Ethan about this and Ethan was right. He needed to get his act together. "I'm fine."

"Good, paste a smile back on your face and let's get back to work."

Logan went back to researching a lead he had, and he made a few phone calls, trying to track down some additional information. Later, when the others started packing up to go home, he stayed.

"Logan, you are calling it a day?" Ethan asked.

"Yeah, I just need a few more minutes to wrap up these notes, you go ahead, I'll lock up."

Ethan hesitated, but left.

Logan waited until everyone had gone. He took out his phone and looked at the message from Sean again. Jerry Townsend. Logan typed the name into his computer and started doing a little digging. He found the arrest record from Roanoke when Blake filed a complaint of domestic assault against him and the record of their divorce and the restraining orders; he checked to see if she had filed one locally. She hadn't, probably hoping she wouldn't need to. It looked like Jerry had lost his job before the divorce, and since then had been working in low-level accounting jobs for small companies. He imagined Jerry was angry, and he hoped the guy was getting help and not planning on doing anything else stupid. It looked like he was paying Blake monthly for the next couple of years, and she had received half the funds from the sale of their house. He was proud of her. Blake had stuck it to the bastard for the way he treated her. He wondered for a dark moment what Blake would do if Jerry showed up here. Was she capable of violence? He didn't think so, but Jerry had spent years controlling her. Then he hit her and now she was free. If Jerry was in town and threatened that freedom, what would she be capable of?

He picked up the phone and sent her a quick text.

"You okay?"

"Yes, heading home from work."

"Okay, be careful. Will call later."

"Okay."

He sat back and stared at the screen. He wondered where Jerry was staying while he was in town. It had to be close and inexpensive. But that still left a dozen cheap motels in the area. He took a drive to satisfy his curiosity. He started with the motels closest to downtown. There were several that were on the local police department's radar for drugs and prostitution. The Neptune was his first stop; it was a holdover from the nineteen sixties, one level, flat roofed building close to the road. Potholes filled the parking lot. The sign out front was still the old-style neon with half the letters burned out. Guest parking was in front of the rooms, which made it easy for him to cruise through looking for the car Jerry had rented. He swung around back where the truckers parked to make sure he had missed nothing before moving on the next.

Logan spent the next several hours cruising the parking lots of Gates Point's less attractive motels. A couple of them were already being visited by the local police. He shook his head. He thought about Blake's view of Gates Point from the magazine article and it was right, Gates Point was a beautiful place. But it was like any other city, large or small, it had the part of town you didn't write about in garden magazines with pretty pictures. He hoped Blake never had to experience this part of the city. And he was hunting a man who had lost everything, he still had more than most people had and he still wasn't happy, he couldn't see beyond his own selfish needs.

Logan drove around until well after midnight. He even drove by the bookstore, knowing it would be closed. But he wanted to see if Jerry was casing it for a future visit. Nothing. Logan then drove over to Blake's apartment; he didn't intend on calling her he hoped she was asleep. He slowly drove through the parking lot; he didn't see anything suspicious. He left and parked across the street. He watched cars driving by; he used his binoculars for any cars pulling into the complex. Until finally he decided he was being ridiculous about the whole thing and drove home. When had he turned into a stalker? He and Blake weren't even a 'thing' nothing romantic had happened between them and he was already acting like a jealous boyfriend. He really needed to get a hold of himself.

***

The weather promised rain, so Blake had driven to work instead of walking like she normally did. At six o'clock she was ready to go home and curl up with a good book. Out on the sidewalk with the door locked, Blake said goodnight to Becca as she headed up the street. She was almost at her car when she saw Jerry sitting across the street from the parking lot. It was the same car that she had seen when she was with Logan. She stopped in her tracks for a moment. He smiled and waved to her before she ran to her car and locked herself in. She looked back to see him making no attempt to approach her. He just sat watching. Blake pulled out of the parking lot and sped away, checking her review mirror to see if Jerry was following her. She breathed a sigh of relief, but as a precaution she drove around a while before going home. She ran up the steps to her apartment and double locked the door. She didn't turn on any lights and made sure all the blinds and curtains were closed, and the door to the balcony was secure. Then she locked herself in the bathroom. He had found her. Logan had been right; it didn't matter that she left her profession and changed her name, he still found her. She wasn't sure how, but it didn't matter he was there, and he clearly wanted her to know it. She took out her phone and thought about calling Logan. But then decided against it. No, this was her problem, she would not leave one man only to run to another for help. She had come to Gates Point to start over and find herself, and that is just what she was going to do. She knew Logan would help her, but she had to do this on her own. So, she called the police.

"Gates Point Police, how can I help you."

"Yes, my ex-husband is following me what do I need to do to file a restraining order?"

"Ma'am, is this an emergency? Are you safe?"

"No, it is not an emergency. I am safe in my apartment. I had an order against him before I moved here and now, he showed up outside my work tonight."

"Okay, ma'am, remain calm, let me get some information from you. What is his name?"

"Jerry Townsend, he lives in Roanoke."

"Okay, and you have a restraining order against them there?"

"Yes, he hit me. Part of the divorce agreement is that he stay away from me."

"Okay, I can send an officer out to your location."

"Is that necessary? Can't I fill it out online or something?"

"We would like to get a statement from you."

Blake sighed. "Okay," she provided the address and was told an officer would be out to speak with her in about half an hour. She hung up and crept out of the bathroom, checking the window. She didn't see any sign of Jerry, but she left the lights off until the officer arrived, anyway.

The next morning, she overslept and called Wendy.

"Hey, would it be a big deal if I took off today. If I feel this bad tomorrow, I may not be in then either."

"No, it's not a problem, is everything alright?"

"I'm not sure. I don't feel well today. I didn't sleep last night, and I have a terrible headache."

"Sure, no problem. Are you sure it is just a headache, nothing else going on?"

"No, not really. I'll let you know if anything changes."

"Okay, Blake, call me if I can do anything."

"Thanks Wendy, you're the best."

Blake hung up and retrieved a bottle of water, peeking out the window at the parking lot. She didn't see any signs of Jerry. She took a couple of aspirin before going to bed.

She slept until nearly three in the afternoon.

She checked her phone, no messages. It disappointed her to have not heard from Logan, but he was probably busy with a case or something. And it was only Tuesday, he had just spent the weekend with her, he probably needed some space. He seemed like a pretty solitary kind of guy; he was probably recharging his emotional batteries from the weekend.

***

Ethan came in smiling, Logan noticed Ethan was more of a morning person now that he and Kay were living together. "Good morning team, don't forget we are going to the range today to practice before our re-qualify trials next week."

Logan groaned; he had forgotten about the training exercise today. From the sour looks from Jared and Stephanie, it looked like he wasn't the only one.

An hour later they all gathered their gear and drove out to the range. They each checked in with the range master, then went to their assigned lanes. No matter how hard he tried, Blake was still on his mind today. It seemed like the harder he tried not to think about her, the more he thought about her smile, and the look on her face when they were kayaking. He closed his eyes for a moment and pushed her aside and focused on the gun in his hand. He scored high and Ethan seemed pleased. So much so, Ethan sent them all home early as a reward. Logan drove to the bookstore.

Wendy greeted him as he came in. "Hi Logan,"

"Hi Wendy, Blake not here today?"

"No, she called in sick."

"Sick? Did she say what was wrong?"

"She said she didn't sleep well and had a headache, but she might not be in tomorrow either."

Logan thought that was odd. He wasn't aware that she had a condition that caused her to have headaches for two days.

"Logan, I'm probably being overcautious, but I'm worried. I don't think it is just a headache, I think there is something else going on with her." Wendy bit her lower lip, not wanting to drag Logan into the middle of something. She had an overwhelming sense that Blake was in some kind of trouble.

"Do you have anything concrete to go on?"

"No, just a hunch."

"Okay, I'll swing by her place and check on her."

"Thanks, Logan."

Logan pulled his phone out of his pocket on his way back to his truck and called Blake. No answer.

It took all of his self-control not to speed on the way to her apartment. Not seeing Jerry's car, he parked and walked up the stairs, knocked on her door and waited. He thought he heard movement, "Blake, it's Logan."

He heard at least three locks being unlocked. She opened the door slowly.

"Logan, what are you doing here?"

"I stopped by the store to see you and Wendy said you were sick. I came by to make sure it wasn't my cooking."

She looked haggard, but still she smiled at him.

"You okay?" He asked.

"Yeah, I just couldn't sleep, and I have a headache."

"Okay, do you need anything?"

"No, oh I'm sorry come in." She stepped aside and looked out the door before closing it. Logan noticed the curtains were drawn. Was it because of the headache?

"Would you like something to drink?" Blake fussed around.

"No, Blake, I'm fine. Were you sleeping when I knocked?"

"No, I was laying here on the couch,"

"Then why don't you come over here and lay back down, if you don't mind, I'll sit with you for a while?"

"Uh, I'm not much company."

He noticed she was protesting, but not very hard. He thought perhaps she really wanted him to stay but couldn't or wouldn't ask him.

He sat down on the end of the sofa nearest the door. She settled on the other side of him. She sighed, relieved to have Logan between her and the door.

"Put your feet up." Logan reached over and put his arm around her, allowing her to lean into him and put her feet up under the afghan she had pulled over herself. It only took her about five minutes, and she was asleep. He wasn't sure what was going on with Blake, but he had a pretty good idea had to do with her ex-husband. It was just too much of a coincidence for her to call out from work after the run-in with the mysterious car. He sat watching her sleep, vowing to himself that even if they never became romantically involved, he wouldn't let anything ever happened to her. And would take care of Jerry Townsend personally, if given the chance. He sat imagining all the ways Jerry Townsend could disappear if it came to it.

CHAPTER TWELVE

Blake slept better than she had in a long time. When she woke, she was embarrassed to find that her head was in Logan's lap and he was asleep with his head in an awkward position.

As soon as she stirred, he woke up.

"I'm so sorry." She blushed.

"Don't be, you feeling any better?"

"Yes, I am, thank you."

He nodded and looked towards the window even with the curtains drawn he could see that it was light outside. He checked the time. He was going to be late for work.

Blake stood and stretched, "Would you like some coffee?"

He fished his phone out of his pocket. "Yes,"

She padded into the kitchen while he sent Ethan a text saying he would be late. He needed to find out what was going on with Blake. He noticed she did not move to open the curtains.

"I'm sorry I fell asleep like that,"

"What's to be sorry about? You were under the weather, nothing wrong with that."

She gave him a sweet smile. "Thank you."

He shrugged "What are friends for?"

"Well, I rarely sleep on my friends." She laughed.

He laughed with her. "Then I will consider myself extra special."

"You have a way of making me feel," she looked away for a moment, "I don't know, safe?" Her cheeks blushed.

"I'm glad." He watched her and drank a little more coffee because he couldn't think of anything to say, and he needed to do something else with his mouth besides give in to the desire to kiss her.

"Well, I hate to drink and run, but I should probably get to work."

"Oh no, will you be late? Will you get in trouble?"

He laughed and reached across the table and took her hand.

"You worry too much. I'm a big boy and I can handle it." He loved how soft and warm she was.

He dragged his hand away and stood up.

"Will you be okay now?"

"Oh yeah, I'll be fine." She said with too much confidence.

"Okay, I'm a phone call away, even if it is just to talk."

She looked like she wanted to say something, but she bit her lower lip instead while walking him to the door.

He had a random thought, "Uh, I was thinking, it's Valentine's Day this week and I realize we are just friends, but do you want to do something, dinner? Movie night?" He knew he was taking an enormous risk in asking.

"Movie night sounds nice." She smiled up at him.

"Great, we can work out the details later I'll call you."

"Okay." She opened the door.

"Lock up when I leave."

She nodded and did just that.

Logan scanned the parking lot as he walked to his truck. He didn't see Jerry or the rental car. He checked his messages on his phone. There was one from Ethan.

"Everything alright?"

He sent a quick reply, "On my way."

Ethan looked up as Logan breezed into the office.

"Sorry boss,"

"It happens, don't worry about it."

Logan nodded and got to work; Jared and Stephanie looked up, noting that Logan was wearing the same clothes from the day before.

Ethan met their gaze briefly, then redirected his eyes to his ringing phone. He nodded a few times and then thanked the caller and hung up. All eyes turned to him.

"Body showed up in the morgue. It could be related to one of our cases, Logan and Jared. Can you go check it out?"

"Sure," Logan stood up and nodded to Jared. "I'll drive."

Jared followed him out to one of the Chevy Suburban's. They drove in silence for the first ten minutes until Jared couldn't stand it anymore.

"Everything okay, man?"

"Sure, why?" Logan kept his eyes on the road.

"I don't know you tell me; you were late; you are never late and you're wearing the same clothes you had on yesterday," Jared waited for a response when it was obvious Logan wasn't going to explain he pressed on, "Look I know we aren't close like you and Ethan but if you need to talk about...,"

"I appreciate the offer, but I'm good. I had to help a friend out last night."

"Oh, okay." Jared nodded. "I hope your friend is okay."

"I hope so, too." Logan turned into the parking lot and parked.

Dr. Andria Chapman greeted them inside. "Gentlemen, thank you for coming down so quickly. I have the dental records back; he's been in the water at least forty-eight hours. I wanted to double check as his fingerprints."

Jared winced, he hated bodies that are submerged for too long; they bothered him more than other types of cadaver the way the bottom feeders picked at them grossed him out.

"Who is it, Doc?" Logan asked.

"According to the records, it is Anthony Patino."

Logan recognized the name, Mr. Patino was wanted for a host of crimes to include human trafficking.

"How'd he die?" He asked as Dr. Chapman moved around the body.

"Shot in the back of the head."

"So, who took him out?" Jared asked, trying to not focus on the soft tissue areas that were missing, like the eyes.

Logan sighed. "That's a good question. You think he's been in the water a couple of days, huh?"

"Again, my best estimate is forty-eight hours based on the damaged to the body, also he didn't have a gallbladder, so he didn't float to the surface, he was drug up by a fishing net."

Jared dry heaved a little, "Not eating seafood this week."

"Why is that important?" Logan asked Dr. Chapman, ignoring Jared.

"Well, a gall bladder will help a body float to the top, without one it can stay down longer, so he may not have drifted too far, but that may take some time to figure out."

"Thanks, Doc." Logan nodded at Jared and they returned to the suburban.

"So now what?" Jared asked.

"We find out who killed, him."

"Really, do we care? I mean, they did the job for us, right?"

"That's true, they took out a bad guy, but why? Is he being replaced by someone worse, someone who is okay with taking a life to further their own cause?"

"I see your point."

"Just because he was a criminal doesn't mean someone outside a courtroom gets to decide his fate."

"You're right, Logan. Sorry."

Logan nodded and climbed in the vehicle.

"When we get back to the office, research Tony's family, see if they have moved recently, any major changes."

"Okay, will do."

Logan pulled up to the curb and Jared got out, "Where are you going?"

"Going to see who's in charge of human trafficking these days, I'll be back later."

Jared watched Logan pull away from the curb and strode into the office, disappointed that Logan hadn't taken him along.

Ethan looked up. "That was quick."

"Yeah, well, the guy is pretty dead."

"Who was it?"

"Tony Patino."

Ethan looked at him in surprise, "Really?"

"Yeah, Dr. Chapman confirmed it through dental records," Seeing the look on Ethan's face, he explained, "He'd been in the water a while."

Ethan nodded, he understood. "So, where's Logan?"

"Not sure, he dropped me off, told me to do some research, said he was going to go see who was in charge of human trafficking these days, whatever that means."

"Shit!" Ethan picked up the phone and called Logan.

"Watson."

"Logan, where are you going?"

"Gotta talk to a guy, Ethan. I'll be back soon."

"Alone?"

"Yeah, the kid nearly lost it looking at Patino with no eyes, I didn't think a trip to the west side was in his best interest right now."

"I don't care if he got squeamish, you know better than to go down there alone."

"I'll be fine, I have a contact down here."

"I don't like this, Logan."

"I'll be fine, dad." Logan had hung up.

"Hello?" Ethan sat staring at his phone for a minute before putting it down. Ethan dialed another number.

"Tech Support, Greg speaking."

"Greg, it's Ethan Craddock."

"Agent Craddock, nice to hear from you. What can I do for you today?"

"Can you trace a cell phone for me?"

"Sure, provided it is on."

"It should be,"

"Okay, I'm ready for the number."

Ethan gave him Logan's cell number. While ignoring the looks from Stephanie and Jared.

"Got it. That's Agent Watson's phone."

"Yes, it is. Can you send that to my cell phone and keep it active?"

"Sure, should be coming through to you now."

Ethan picked up his cell phone and opened the app that would allow him to track Logan's location. "Got it, thanks." He stood up, heading for the door.

"Uh, boss, do you want one of us to come with you?"

"No, hopefully it will be nothing and I'll be back in a few minutes."

"And if it's not?" Stephanie looked worried.

"Then you two will have to decide who'll be in charge." Ethan wanted to make sure his agent and his friend didn't get himself into trouble. Ethan followed Logan's signal to an area of town that most people avoided. He could see Logan was heading for an abandoned warehouse. The whole industrial park had seen better days. Grass grew through the asphalt in random patches. The chain-link fence was rusted and sagged. He pulled in between two shipping containers to shield himself from Logan's line of sight, then he got out and made his way along the edge of the building. Ethan wanted to be close enough to lend a hand if needed. He positioned himself at a gap in the corrugated metal siding. He tracked Logan's voice, but it took him a minute to find him in the shadows.

The man Logan was talking to was reed thin with a weasel-like face. "I just saw a very dead Patino, in the morgue. You know anything about that, Manny?"

"Why would I know anything?"

"Because, if you don't then you are no longer useful to me."

"Okay, okay. Maybe I heard some things."

"What kind of things, Manny?"

"Like Patino was getting too soft in his old age. Like he wasn't getting any respect anymore,"

Ethan could see that Manny was nervous and twitchy. Was it because he was talking to Logan or something else? He suddenly had a bad feeling about this meeting. Logan's voice carried through the shadows of the warehouse, "Who thought it was time for Patino to go?"

"I don't know," Manny shrugged, "lots of people."

"Okay, who's in charge now? Who's making the decisions at the top?"

Manny looked around nervously.

"You got somewhere you need to be?" Logan asked.

Ethan slipped in a through a broken door and crouched behind some old shipping crates. Manny was clearly getting more and more nervous by the minute. Ethan smelled a setup. He started making his way slowly towards Logan. Logan must have sensed trouble as well because he pulled his handgun and pointed it at Manny. "You set me up, Manny?"

"No, no, I wouldn't do that man!" Logan grabbed Manny by the arm and start steering him towards the door. A shot rang out, and it hit the ground between Logan and the door, stopping him in his tracks. Ethan tried to track where the shot came from, Logan was in the open and exposed.

He put Manny in front of him.

"I got your boy!" Logan called out.

Manny pleaded. "Logan, please!"

"You set me up, why shouldn't I use you as a shield you were willing to sacrifice me."

"Yeah, but you're a cop you can't do this?"

"You're not going to tell anyone, are you? Besides, who's going to miss you?"

Another shot and Manny slumped to the floor. Ethan saw the muzzle flash and returned fire, giving Logan a chance to take cover.

Logan wasn't sure who else was in the warehouse, but there was at least one person on his side. He charged towards the area the gun fire had originated. The bad guy raised up just enough and Logan fired. The silence that followed told him he had hit his mark.

Logan waited a beat, then moved cautiously to confirm the man was down and to see if he needed an ambulance.

Ethan called out, "Logan!"

"Yeah!"

"It's Ethan, coming out."

"Come ahead."

Ethan stepped out from behind the crates to Logan's left. "You okay?"

"I'm fine. You?"

"Fine."

"What are you doing here?"

"I thought you might need some backup."

Logan nodded. "Thanks."

They both looked down at the man. He didn't need an ambulance. But they called one for both victims, anyway.

Ethan looked around, "You find anything useful?"

Logan nodded, "an insider, someone younger killed Patino."

When Logan finally made it home, he checked to see if there were any messages from Blake. None. He sent her a text and waited. It was an hour later before his phone rang.

He answered, "Logan."

"It's Blake." Her voice a whisper.

He sat straight up in his chair. "What's wrong?"

"I think there is someone outside my door, just standing there."

"Can you see who it is through the peephole?"

"No, I think they covered it."

"I'm on my way. Did you call the police?"

"No, what would I tell them?"

"Tell them someone is trying to break into your apartment."

"Okay."

"Blake, call me back after you call them, okay?"

"I will."

Logan ran to his truck and sped to Blake's apartment. He pulled in the parking lot slowly and turned off the lights. His phone rang.

"Blake?"

"Yeah, are you close?"

"I'm downstairs, is he still there?"

"Yes."

"Are the police on the way?"

"Yes, but it will be a while they didn't think it was an emergency."

"Okay, that's fine. Stay on the line." He put his earpiece in and pocketed the phone. He crept around the back of the apartment and listened. There was definitely someone up there. He slowly inched towards the stairs leading up. There was no cover; no way to conceal himself, whoever it was would see him coming as soon as he started up. He would have to run up hard and fast. There was no place for the stalker to go but to the third level.

Logan pulled his Sig Sauer and drew in a breath. "Blake, you with me?"

"Yes."

"Go to the bedroom and shut the door. Stay away from the front of the apartment."

"Okay."

He ran up the stairs, "Hold it right there, don't move! FBI!"

Jerry Townsend jumped; he tried to run, but Logan was on him too quickly.

"Come here, you son of a bitch!" Logan grabbed him by the collar and drug him back down the stairs. "What are you doing outside this apartment?"

"I live here I forgot my keys."

"Bullshit! Let's have some ID."

"You have no right!" Jerry protested.

"Really? You think so? Did you not hear me say FBI? Do you not see this badge?" Logan pointed to the badge in the leather case hanging from his neck on a chain.

Jerry's hands shook as he handed his ID to Logan.

"Says here Mr. Townsend that you live in Roanoke. That's not really near here, is it?"

"Not really."

"So, you want to tell me again what you are doing here?"

"I don't have to tell you anything!"

"Listen asshole, I've already killed one man today, it really wouldn't be ruining my day to kill another one, got it?"

"Are you threatening me?"

"No sir, stating facts. I believe it is you who is doing the threatening tonight. Now I'll ask you again, what are you doing here at this address?"

"Visiting a friend."

"And do you always put electrical tape over the peepholes of your friends' apartments?"

"I... I,"

"Yeah, right?"

"Police! Stay right there!"

"FBI!" Logan answered.

"Put down your weapon."

Logan laid the gun on the top step. He didn't let go of Jerry.

Jerry started screaming, "This man assaulted me."

The officer looked at Logan and his ID and then at Jerry.

"I doubt it."

Logan handed the officer Jerry's ID.

"Mr. Townsend, who are you visiting here tonight?"

"A friend."

"Does your friend have a name?"

"Blake Townsend, Morgan" He corrected himself.

"Is that right? And where is Ms. Morgan now?"

"She didn't answer the door. I assume she is home." He nodded in the direction of the Blake's apartment door.

"Mr. Townsend, you are in violation of a restraining order, you need to come with me."

"What?" He looked from the officer to Logan. Logan smiled.

"Have a pleasant night, Mr. Townsend, and remember what I said."

After the police officer left, Logan peeled the tape off the door. "Blake, you still with me?"

"Yes," she whispered.

"He's gone."

"Thank you," she paused. "Is what you said to Jerry true?"

Logan hung his head; he knew what she was talking about.

"Did you really kill someone today?" she asked.

"Unfortunately, yes, I did. The man I shot today, had already killed another man right in front of me. I didn't want to do it, but I had little choice." He hoped she understood. But he wouldn't blame her if she didn't.

"Okay." She answered. He waited, but after a long pause it was clear she wasn't going to invite him in. Just as well.

"Call me if you need anything, Blake. I'm here for you."

"Okay, thank you."

He listened for another minute and then disconnected the call. He walked back to his truck feeling more tired than he had ever had in his life.

Ethan looked up when Logan came in to work earlier than usual. "Logan, you look like death warmed over, why don't you take the day and get some sleep."

"I'm fine."

"Yeah, I was fine like that once." Ethan returned to the file on his desk, giving Logan his space.

CHAPTER THIRTEEN

Wendy arrived early to open up the store. She hadn't heard from Blake and didn't want to assume she would be back to work today. So, she was surprised to find Blake working at the table in the back room.

"Morning Blake," Wendy greeted.

"Morning, Wendy. Listen, I'm sorry about the past couple of days."

"It's okay, really." Seeing Blake, Wendy got the sense there was more going on than just her being under the weather. "Is everything alright?"

Blake looked like she was going to say something but changed her mind. She looked at Wendy and a tear escaped down her cheek. "Not really."

"Oh my gosh, come here!" Wendy pulled her in for a hug. "Tell me what is going on?"

"My ex-husband found me and has been following me."

"Did you call the police?"

"Yes, and I took out a restraining order, again. But they don't help. They never help."

"Okay, so then what happened?"

"Like I said, those orders don't help. Last night he came to my apartment and put tape on the door so I couldn't see out and then just stood there for like an hour and wouldn't leave."

Wendy was stunned. "That's horrible!"

"I called the police, but they said it was going to take them a while to get to me and to stay locked in my apartment. But I was so scared." Blake trembled.

"Of course, you were!"

"I called Logan."

"You did?"

"Yeah, and he got there before the police."

Wendy wanted to ask if her ex was still in one piece, but she held her tongue.

"Logan got there, he must have grabbed Jerry or something because I could hear a scuffle and then Logan told him he had killed one person already and that he would kill him too, if he didn't leave me alone. The police came and arrested Jerry."

Blake was hyperventilating.

"Come sit down," Wendy steered her to a chair.

"So that is good right, they arrested your ex."

"Yeah, that part is good."

Blake was clearly upset, but it didn't seem to be about her ex-husband. "The restraining order worked, they arrested him, right?"

"Do you think Logan really killed someone yesterday?"

Wendy pulled back a little and stared at Blake. She was more upset about Logan than her own safety or that of her ex.

"I suppose it is possible. What did Logan say about it? Did you ask him?"

"I did over the phone. He said that he shot a man who had killed someone earlier in the day."

"Okay, well, that sounds like a really difficult situation, but it also sounds like Logan didn't have a choice. What else did he say?"

"Nothing, I was afraid. I was afraid to let him in my apartment after that."

Wendy looked at Blake, stunned. Her heart broke a little for Logan. She wondered how he felt today. "Oh Blake, you have to know Logan would never hurt you or anyone that wasn't a threat to someone else, you know, that right? He is an FBI agent sometimes these things happen. It's his job."

"I know, I know." Blake cried. "I feel horrible. I knew it in the back of my mind that it was part of his job but, I didn't grasp the reality of it until last night."

"Were you worried for Jerry's safety?"

Blake looked up, "No, I worried about what it would do to Logan to have to kill Jerry."

"I think you need to have a chat with Logan."

"I can't, I'm too ashamed about the way I acted last night."

"You have to. He's probably upset with himself and the situation that caused him to have to take a life. Now he is probably hurting, thinking you have rejected him."

"Oh god!" Blake put her head in her hands.

"Blake, you need to go see him and I mean right now."

"Okay, okay. You're right. But I don't know where his office is."

"Come on, we'll find it." Wendy walked over to the computer to look up the address of the Gates Point FBI field office. "You go freshen up; I'll get the address."

Blake nodded and rushed to the bathroom to wash her face.

Wendy was waiting for her when she returned.

"Better?"

"Yes, thank you."

"Okay, here is the address. Text him and tell him you're on your way, but you need to go talk to him."

"Are you sure about this?" Blake wasn't sure this was a good idea. What if Logan wasn't upset? What if he didn't care for her the same way, she cared about him? And exactly how much did she care? Her heart was pounding, and her mind was reeling. "Wendy, I don't know about this."

"Look, you were upset about all night, right?"

"Yes,"

"Then ago explain, or apologize, if you think you need to or thank him for coming to the rescue. It will give you a chance to see how he is feeling about it today and no matter what happens you will have dealt with it." Wendy took Blake's shoulders and steered her towards the door. "Don't come back until it's done."

Blake swallowed hard and nodded. "Okay."

She watched Blake walk down the sidewalk to her car.

***

Logan's phone buzzed with a text message.

"Do you have a minute to talk?"

He replied, "Yes."

He sat waiting for the phone to ring. The security guard opened the door, "Agent Watson, you have a visitor."

Everyone looked up as Blake walked into the room wearing jeans and a pink angora sweater; she` looked around nervously. Logan stood up.

"Blake is everything alright?"

Everyone staring at her intimidated Blake. "I'm sorry to bother you, do you have a minute?"

"Sure, come with me." He led her to the conference room, closing the door and the blinds.

Ethan watched with interest as the couple disappeared.

"What is that all about?" Jared wondered aloud.

"No idea." Ethan answered, wondering the same thing.

Logan looked at Blake he could tell she had been crying.

"Are you okay?" He wanted to touch her but forced himself to stay out of reach.

"Not really." Blake shook her head and looked away. She fought back more tears. "I came to apologize."

Logan wasn't sure what he was expecting Blake to say, but it wasn't an apology. "Apologize for what?"

"For last night."

Logan nodded, clearly. She regretted getting him involved last night and he couldn't blame her, he probably took it too far. "That was my fault I shouldn't...."

Blake cut him off by raising her hand. "Let me finish."

"I'm sorry for the way I acted last night. I don't know why I responded that way. I am so grateful to you. You came and rescued me and I..." She fought back the tears of shame.

Logan's heart cracked at the knowledge she was so upset. He stepped closer and took her hands. Blake continued to stare at the floor.

"Hey," Logan whispered. He bent down to see her face. "Hey, you don't have to apologize." He put his forefinger under her chin gently.

She looked up at him.

"Blake, I'm sorry. I shouldn't have let you hear all of that. It's probably good that you find out now what kind of person I am."

"I know what kind of person you are." She said defiantly.

"Yeah, and what kind is that?"

"The kind who comes when a friend calls needing help. The kind of man who befriends a stranger, a gentleman. A person who cares about others so much they would do anything for them."

He blinked at her. He finally found his words, "I'd never do anything to hurt you or scare you."

She nodded. "I know that, I do. I don't understand what I was thinking last night."

"It scared you, that is okay, too."

"I am ashamed of my behavior; I must have seen like some psycho ungrateful person."

"No, you didn't. You needed to protect yourself. That is normal, and I'm glad you did it. I realize you aren't so trusting you would let a crazy person in your apartment."

She laughed a little. "No, I wouldn't. But I will always let you in."

"You do what makes you feel safe, don't worry about me."

"But I worry about you. I care about you." She met his gaze.

He studied her face, trying to determine the meaning behind her words.

"I care for you too." He smiled at her.

His smile had a way of making her knees turn to jello.

She nodded, "Okay, well, I'm glad we got that straight."

"Me too."

"Uh, I should probably get back to work." She suddenly was feeling awkward.

"Yeah, me too." Logan didn't move. He stood staring down at her. "Why don't I introduce you to the team before you go." He walked her out, everyone in the room was trying to look busy. He shook his head.

"Everyone, I'd like to introduce a friend of mine,"

Ethan, Jared, and Stephanie all looked up at once. Ethan came forward first.

Logan smiled at Blake, "This is Ethan, my boss."

"Hi Blake," Ethan stretched out his hand.

"Hi, I've heard a lot about you." Blake smiled.

"Ut Oh, boss." Jared laughed, stepping forward.

"Hi, I'm Jared."

"A pleasure to meet you." Blake smiled.

"And I'm Stephanie,"

"Hi," Blake shook hands with Jared and Stephanie.

"Come on, I'll walk you to your car." Logan nodded to the team.

"Okay." Blake smiled up at him. "It was nice to meet you all."

"Come back anytime." Jared called out.

"Yeah, it would be nice to have another girl around once in a while." Stephanie smiled.

Blake followed Logan outside.

"Your friends are all really nice."

"Yeah, they are alright."

Blake laughed. "Ethan, is nearly as intimidating as you."

"You think I am intimidating?"

"Well, Logan, I mean, even before last night, you come across as kind of badass."

"Really?"

"You don't think so?"

"Well, I hadn't given it much thought."

"Don't worry it suits you very well."

"Not if it scares you."

"I didn't say that." She winked at him.

He couldn't help himself as he grinned at her.

"I'll talk to you later, okay?" She said opening her car door.

"Okay, be careful. Call me if you need me."

"I will." And she meant it.

He watched her go and walked back inside. The team was standing where he had left them.

"What?"

"Nothing," Ethan smiled and returned to his desk.

"She's really nice." Stephanie smiled.

"You should invite her to come out with us." Jared suggested.

"We're just friends." Logan argued.

Everyone laughed and shook their heads, not believing him for a minute. Ethan watched Logan carefully. Logan's mood clearly changed after Blake left. Whatever had been on his mind was erased by her visit. He knew what Logan was going through. Logan had been there for him when he went through the same roller coaster of emotions over Kay last year. He had kept his distance while giving Ethan plenty of space to work out his problems.

They all worked late into the evening, and Ethan finally sent them home. Logan was the last to leave, as usual.

"Got time for a drink tonight?" Ethan asked.

"Yeah, I think so. What did you have in mind?"

"How about the Ironclad? Not too loud, not too slow."

"Sure, meet you there." Logan nodded and left.

Ethan sent a text message to Kay, "Having a beer with Logan, tonight."

"Okay, have fun." Came the reply.

Logan was sitting at the bar when Ethan arrived.

"Hey man," Ethan slapped Logan on the back.

"Hey, what's up?"

The bartender brought Ethan a beer.

"Just thought I'd check in with you; see what's going on."

"This is about Blake coming to the office, isn't it?"

"No, this is about you looking like hell, being surly and then doing a one eighty after she leaves."

"I didn't get any sleep last night."

"Because of the shooting?"

"No, although that was pretty messed up. I made a mistake going down there alone. But you knew that already."

"Why do you think I followed you?"

Logan laughed and drained his beer.

"No, after that Blake called. Her ex-husband has been hanging around. She has a restraining order, but that doesn't seem to matter." He nodded as the bartender brought him a refill, "So anyway last night she calls me because he is standing outside her apartment door and put tape over the peephole so she can't see him. She flipped out. I was talking to her on the phone and didn't hang up before I reached the guy, so she heard everything I said to him."

"What did you say?"

"I told him I'd killed one man already that day and I wouldn't be bothered by killing another."

"Whoa!"

"Yeah, I think that freaked her out even more than the stalker ex-husband. She refused to talk to me after that, much less let me in to check on her."

"So, what happened?"

"The cops came and arrested him, and I drove home."

Ethan nodded, "That is a pretty messed up night."

"Yeah, it was. Today she wanted to tell me she was sorry for not talking to me and to reassure me she doesn't think I am a monster," Logan shook his head in dismay, "I have to tell you last night, I sure felt like one."

Ethan understood what Logan meant. The job was the job and some days you have to do things or see things you hope most people never have to see or deal with, and you don't want to take that home to your family. It makes you feel dirty somehow. He had struggled with that in his first marriage. It was a little different with Kay she understood it better than most people and it helped him get through the tough days.

"Logan, I have to ask you something,"

Logan nodded for Ethan to continue.

"Do you love this woman? Do you see your life without her in it?"

"I can't imagine not seeing her every day."

"Okay, I get that each person, each couple deals with things differently but let me tell you it can be hard for the other person when they don't understand, really understand what we do and why. I know most days aren't like yesterday. But there are enough of those days that happen, and that caused my first marriage to end. I don't want to see that happen to you. I don't have any answers about how to deal with it," Ethan put his hand on Logan's shoulder, "you need to know her side of things too."

Logan nodded. "I hear what you're saying, but we aren't even dating."

"Really? If you didn't care about her, last night would have been no big deal and she wouldn't have come to the office today to see you." Ethan smiled. "You kids take it slow. No need to rush things. Just realize her side of it too," Ethan threw some bills down on the bar, slapped Logan on the shoulder and left.

CHAPTER FOURTEEN

The bell on the door jingled signaling a customer, Wendy looked up.

"Hello and welcome. Let me know if you need help finding anything."

"Actually, I'm looking for Blake is she working today?"

"She will be in shortly; can I help you with something specific in the meantime?"

"No, I'll wait." The man looked around, "Is there anyone else here?"

"No," Wendy was getting a bad vibe from this customer. She inched closer to the phone behind the counter. The conversation with Blake about her ex-husband stalking her replayed in her mind.

"What are you doing?"

"Nothing, why?" Wendy froze, certain now that something bad was about to happen.

"I saw you move!" He pointed at her, then looked out the window. He was tracking something in the street. Then suddenly he pulled a gun from his waistband and pointed it at Wendy.

"Come on, let's go!"

"Where?"

"Is there a storeroom or something?"

"Yes,"

"Show me and don't try anything." He waived the gun at her.

She led him to the backroom of the store used for sorting incoming books. "Okay, give me your cell phone!"

Wendy fished it out of her jeans pocket and handed it to him. He tossed it in a mop bucket in the corner. "Now stay quiet."

Wendy stood frozen in place; she was so scared she didn't think her legs would move even if she wanted them to. She trembled and tried to imagine what this man wanted.

"If you want money, it is up front in the register,"

"Shut up!"

Blake walked to work that morning feeling better about her and Logan. He had texted her when he got home after work.

Wendy wasn't at the counter when she walked in, "I'm here!" she called out.

"I'm back here!" Wendy answered.

"Okay." Blake put her purse away and walk to the back of the store to check on Wendy. She stopped in her tracks at the sight of Wendy standing in the workroom all the color drained from her face; and Jerry was standing behind her holding a gun.

"Jerry, what the hell are you doing?" She screamed.

"Getting your attention,"

"Really, you had my attention for six years and you blew it, and now you want it? Why?"

"Because you ruined my life," He yelled and pushed the gun closer to Wendy.

"So, pointing a gun at her, does what? Why don't you let her go and I'll give you my undivided attention?"

"No!"

Blake's heart raced, and her palms were sweating. She didn't believe he would hurt Wendy; he wanted her, and she knew it. She couldn't let anything happen to Wendy. "Fine, then I'm leaving."

"I'll shoot her!"

"You're waving a gun around because you want my attention, now you have it. Do you need to keep pointing the gun at her?" She could see the wheels spinning in his mind. "Let me help you with the answer, you don't. Let Wendy go and you and I can talk. Unless you want her to hear all our business."

Jerry growled, "She stays!"

"Okay so you want her to hear how you were a control freak, or a womanizer, or the part where you got fired for what was it again?" She should have been frightened, but she wasn't. She was angry.

"Fine!" He shoved Wendy forward. "Get out and lock up the store!"

Wendy looked at Blake, "Don't do this!"

"It's okay Wendy, do as he says. Close the store and leave," Blake grabbed her arm, "I'm so sorry."

Wendy nodded and ran out of the store as quickly as she could. She rushed into the shop next door, "Please, I need to use your phone!" The clerk recognized Wendy and nodded. Wendy grabbed the phone and dialed.

"Agent Watson,"

"Logan! It's Wendy,"

Logan stood up, alarmed at the sound of Wendy's voice, drawing the attention of the team.

"Wendy, what's wrong?"

"A man," her voice trembled "A man came in the store with a gun. He has Blake, and he's barricaded inside!"

"Is it her ex-husband?"

"I think so."

"Wendy, listen to me. I want you to hang up and call the police, I'm on my way." Logan was already rushing for the door.

Ethan and the team followed him. Ethan caught up to Logan and climbed into the SUV next to him.

"Boss?"

"We're all going,"

Logan didn't argue he just put it in drive and sped out of the parking lot.

"You want to tell me about this guy?" Ethan asked.

"Her ex, she divorced him after he hit her. So much for that restraining order."

Ethan nodded and relayed the information to Jared and Stephanie in the SUV behind them. "You do understand we have to let the local police take the lead on this, right?" Ethan asked.

Logan nodded.

"Logan, I'm serious you can't just kick the door in and go after this guy."

"I hear you,"

"Do you?"

Ethan doubted it, he'd seen that look in Logan's eye before, in the mirror. He had that look once, too, when Kay had been in danger. Logan had physically restrained him. Ethan wasn't sure he could stop Logan.

They pulled over to the curb a block from the bookstore. The local police were already there. Logan was out of the SUV, heading over to the uniformed officers.

He flashed his badge, "Who's in charge?"

"I am!" A uniformed sergeant called out.

"Agent Watson, what information do we have?"

The sergeant nodded, "Only what the bookstore owner told us when we got here, a customer came in, forced her to the rear of the store at gunpoint, demanding to know the location of an employee by the name of," He checked his notes, "Blake Morgan. When Ms. Morgan arrived, he let the store owner go and barricaded himself and Ms. Morgan in the store."

"Have you had communication with him yet?"

"No,"

"Okay, well, I can tell you the man inside is likely to be Jerry Townsend, Ms. Morgan's ex-husband. He was arrested two nights ago outside her apartment for violating a restraining order."

"And you know this how?"

"I'm a friend of Ms. Morgan's and I was there when he was arrested."

"I see,"

"No, I don't think you do,"

"Logan!" Ethan put a hand on Logan's arm, "Why don't we let them do their job first, and then I'm sure if they need our help they will ask, won't you sergeant?"

"Yeah, sure."

Ethan walked Logan away, "Listen, they have a job to do, okay?"

"No, it's not okay. I want to go in there and beat the little shit!"

"Yeah, sure you do, but the focus right now is getting Blake out safely. Then we can decide if you get to give the guy a beat down or not."

Logan was pumped up and not willing to listen to reason. He wanted to punch something, badly. Jerry Townsend was the only thing that would do.

"Come on, let's take a walk," Ethan steered Logan away, they walked back to the trucks, "Jared, monitor the local PD, if you think they need our help or things look like they are about to go south you call me." Ethan tapped his year piece.

"You got it, boss."

"Ethan," Logan protested.

"Look, you need to just chill out a minute. Take it down a notch or you're going to make the situation worse."

"I don't like feeling like this!"

Ethan looked at him curiously, "Like what?"

"Helpless, angry! Is this how you feel because of Kay? If this is what being in love with someone feels like, I don't want any part of it."

Ethan held up his hands in mock surrender. "Whoa big guy, look yes, sometimes you get angry and think you are helpless and a hundred other things when someone you care about is hurting or in trouble, its natural and there isn't a damn thing you can do about it."

"I can walk away; I don't like how this makes me feel. I can't handle not being able to do anything about it."

"Can you really just walk away?" Ethan knew the answer even if Logan didn't at that moment, "Because if you can, do it now, save yourself and her the heartache later, we will all get back in the SUV's and let the police handle this, it's none of our business, yet."

Logan stood there staring, Ethan could see the wheels turning in his head. For a minute he thought Logan might actually leave, but in the end, Logan shook his head and swore.

"Well, I sure as shit can't stand here and watch these guys muck it up."

"So, what do you want to do? Pull rank? Step on some local police department toes and do what? I will not let you kick the door in any more than they will."

Logan shouted. "What am I supposed to do, Ethan?"

"You need to let those guys over there do their job, then you and Blake need to determine how much you love each other."

"You didn't have to decide how you felt about Kay. You knew it from the moment you saw her."

"That's true, but if you remember I was also very married at the time and it was six years before I saw Kay again. Do you want to relive my life, or learn from it?"

Logan ran his hand through his hair and blew out a breath. Shaking his head, he looked at Ethan, "I don't know. But I can't take this."

The sound of a police bullhorn drew Ethan's attention away from Logan.

"Mr. Townsend, this is the Gates Point Police, we are going to call you on the store's phone, please answer it."

Ethan looked back at Logan, then drifted towards the police gathered across the street from the bookstore.

Brian Newsome, Gates Point's hostage negotiator, was standing behind a marked police car holding a cell phone in one hand, a bullhorn in the other.

"Brian," Ethan said as he approached.

"Hey, Ethan, just a minute." Brian held the cell phone up to his ear and waited.

"Jerry, can I call you Jerry?" There was a pause, "I'm sergeant Brian Newsome with the Gates Point police department, can you tell me how you're doing today?"

Ethan watched and listened. He had worked with Brian before and respected his abilities to talk someone down out of a dangerous situation. Ethan looked over his shoulder to see Logan pacing up and down the sidewalk. He understood how Logan felt. He more than understood what it was like to want to do everything possible to rescue the person you cared about, only to be forced to let someone else handle it. It was torture.

"Okay, I hear what you are saying, and I'm divorced myself. Relationships are hard, Jerry I'm sure you don't want to hurt Blake, do you?"

"No, I don't but I want her to comprehend how much I still love her!" Jerry was yelling into the phone, while he pointed the gun at Blake. She sat frozen in place watching Jerry, a man she once loved, coming completely apart. She believed with all of her heart she did the right thing by leaving him. She could not stay with a man who hit her because it would only get worse and clearly, he was capable of much more.

"Jerry, please!"

"Shut up!" He yelled at her, then returned his attention back to Brian Newsome. "Blake's fine, and she'll be better once she comes home where she belongs." He hung up.

Brian stared at his phone for a minute. He looked up at Ethan, "I don't think I'm getting through to him. He is delusional. He believes that if he can get Blake to leave with him, then everything will be fine."

"We can't let that happen, Brian."

"I know that, Ethan. I need to get some eyes in there and see what is going on. There is no way he is going to let her go."

Logan walked over to join Ethan and Brian, "What's happening?"

"Jerry thinks Blake goes back home, then things return to normal."

"That will not happen."

Ethan held his hands up towards Logan, "We get that, so just calm down."

Logan looked over Ethan's shoulder at Brian, who nodded in return.

Logan looked at the store. "Do we know where in the store they are located?"

"No, and whatever you're thinking, forget it!" Ethan said.

Logan looked around and spotted Wendy. He strode in her direction without another word to Ethan.

Brian looked over at Ethan, "Is there something I should know about here?"

"He has been sort of dating the victim."

"You need to get him out of here, right now!"

Ethan sighed heavily, "yeah, you're right." But he made no move towards Logan.

Brian tried dialing the store's number again.

"Wendy!"

Wendy rushed over and threw her arms around Logan, "I'm so glad you are here!"

"Wendy, can you draw me a sketch of the store, any skylights, windows in the back, other ways a person could get in or out?"

"What are you going to do, Logan?"

"Get her out!"

"Okay," Wendy nodded and found a piece of paper and a pen. She gave him the layout. "The last time I saw them they were in the very back, in this room here," She pointed on the paper.

"Okay, that's good. Thanks!" Logan looked around to see if Ethan was still talking to Detective Newsome. He he could guess where Jared and Stephanie were at, but he assumed they were somewhere in the crowd of cops. He walked casually to the end of the building that included the bookstore and ducked down the alley. Each business had a deliver door with their name stenciled on it and he jogged up the alley until he got to Bumboat Books. Wendy had given him the key to the deadbolt. Logan carefully turned the lock. He put his ear to the door and listened. He couldn't hear anything and reconsidered his options for a moment. He heard a phone ringing, it sounded like it was in another room and not near the door, then he heard a very muffled voice. This was his chance. Jerry was distracted. He could only hope that Jerry's line of sight was obstructed. Logan eased the door open. He slipped in, closing the door behind him. He pulled out his 9mm Sig Sauer and listened. It sounded like Jerry was up front. He crept through the room, carefully staying out of sight. Once he left the workroom, there wouldn't be much cover and he would have to act quickly if Jerry saw him.

He also needed to act before the local police did anything like tear gas the store. He didn't have a radio or earbud with him, so he couldn't stop them if they made a forcible entry.

Outside Ethan was getting impatient, "What's the plan, Brian?"

"We need eyes inside, I'm not sure how we can do that, for now I have someone getting out the thermal device so we can at least see where they are in the store."

Ethan nodded that was a good plan, that would at least help them figure out where they could make entry safely if Brian couldn't talk Jerry out.

Brian dialed the phone again and waited for Jerry to pick up.

"Jerry, it's Brian Newsome again. Everything still okay in there?"

"Yeah, we're fine, but I want you to back off, Blake and I are leaving, and I don't want anyone to stop us."

"Okay, I hear you Jerry, but there are a lot of people worried about Blake out here. It is going to take me a few minutes to convince them they need to leave. In the meantime, why don't you tell me about why you are here today."

"I already told you, Blake is going home with me. Everything will be alright if she just comes back home."

"Okay, why are things not alright at home. Why did Blake leave?"

Brian could hear Jerry breathing heavy, he was obviously upset and there was a long pause.

"Jerry, what happened that made Blake want to leave?"

"I hit her! Okay? I didn't mean to, but I hit her!" Jerry was shouting and Brian feared things would go either way at this point.

"Detective, we have three heat signatures in the building."

"What?"

Ethan looked over at the screen. Logan.

"Who the hell is the third person?" Brian asked, looking at the officer. Brian raised the phone and Ethan feared he was going to alert Jerry of another person in the store. He reached out and touched Brian's arm.

"Wait,"

Brian lowered the phone.

Ethan sighed and looked around, "I think its Logan, just give me a minute and don't mention it to anyone. Not yet."

Brian scowled and nodded. Ethan began looking for Logan, he spotted Jared. "Hey, have you seen Logan?"

"Saw him walking down the block a few minutes ago."

"That way?" Ethan pointed.

"Yeah, boss, what's going on?"

"Gear up, I think Logan is inside the store with the gunman."

Jared flagged down Stephanie and they jogged to the SUV's and got their tech gear and vests.

Ethan jogged back over to Brian, "I'm pretty sure Logan is in there and he doesn't have his vest or his radio."

"That's pretty stupid."

"Yeah, it is."

Brian got on his radio, "Okay team listen up, we have a federal agent inside the building. We do not believe the gunman is aware of his presence, let's try to keep everyone alive today."

Brian turned to Ethan, "You've got to be kidding me. What the hell is your guy thinking? Now I have two potential hostages to deal with!"

"He isn't thinking that's the problem. He has a thing for Blake and he's already had run-ins with this guy Jerry."

"Then he shouldn't even be on the scene, Ethan." Brian ran his hand over his head in frustration.

"I know, I know, and I take full responsibility." Ethan waved over his shoulder as he strode away in the direction of his team.

Brian called out. "You damn well better if this goes south it isn't going to be my head on the chopping block."

Ethan turn to face him. "I'll make sure it isn't."

Stephanie and Jared joined Ethan. "So, what do we do, boss?"

Ethan glanced at Brian, "Stay out of PD's way, but make sure our boy doesn't get shot. We don't have a way to communicate with him."

"Can't we call him?" Stephanie asked.

"Can't risk that is phone won't give him away."

"What about a text?"

"Okay Stephanie, let's try to text him."

Logan's phone vibrated in his pocket. It had to be Ethan and frankly he was surprised it took him this long to realize he was in the store. He read the message.

"Confirm, you are inside."

"Yes,"

"You have eyes on?"

"No,"

Stephanie walked over and took a picture of the thermal imaging screen and sent it to Logan.

"Thank you,"

If Jerry move towards the back of the store. He wanted to get Blake's attention and reassure her everything was going to be okay.

Logan heard Blake's voice. "Jerry, why are you doing this? Do you really think I am going to go home with you?"

"Yes, we can make this right. We can make it the way it used to be."

"Jerry, even if the cops let you walk out of here scot free, I am not going anywhere with you ever again!"

Logan wished Blake would stop talking. She was making the situation worse, and Jerry's mood was escalating.

"Yes, you will!"

"No, I won't. That part of my life is over, you blew it! Where do you get off acting like the injured party here? If your life blew up Jerry, it's because you lit the fuse."

"You didn't give me a chance to make it right!"

"You can't take something like that back, Jerry. I'm not one of those women who lets her husband smack her around and then accepts his apology."

"You don't believe I would ever hurt you, do you?"

"You already did!" Blake screamed. "All the years of you keeping tabs on me when I was out with my girlfriends, how much money I spent, then it only escalated to you hitting me and now this!"

"No, no, no!" Jerry began pacing. When he walked away from Blake, Logan stuck his head around the corner of a bookshelf to get Blake's attention. She saw him and sucked in a breath.

"What?" Jerry rushed back over to her.

"Nothing, you're scaring me and hurting me again!"

"I haven't hurt anyone!"

"You scared Wendy half to death, and you have her shop closed to business, the cops are outside, you think anyone is enjoying this? Are you?"

"No, I just want us to go home and things to be the way they used to be." He held both hands up to his head in frustration. He was on the verge of losing it, Logan had to be ready to act fast. Jerry started pacing again, this time once he was far enough away from Blake, Logan stepped out of the shadows.

"Freeze, don't move!"

Jerry froze, more out of shock than in compliance with Logan's words.

Logan pointed at Blake without taking his eyes off Jerry, "Blake, go out the back door."

"No!" Jerry pointed his gun at Blake. Logan started drifting towards Blake to put himself between her and Jerry.

"Jerry," Logan kept his voice calm, "You need to focus on me, not her, I'm the one with the gun. I'm the one that will kill you if I believe for one second you are going to pull that trigger. Nod if you understand."

Jerry nodded slowly, but his eyes locked on Blake. Logan slid his finger to the trigger of his gun. He wouldn't give Jerry a reason to shoot, but he needed to protect Blake.

"Jerry, look at me."

Jerry didn't take his eyes off Blake as he swung his weapon around towards Logan. Logan fired one shot and Jerry dropped to the floor. Blood flowing from his head.

Logan knew the local police would crash through the door any second with their weapons drawn. He could only hope that the thermal imaging camera told them what they needed to know. Still, he rushed over and wrapped his arms around Blake, turning his back to the front door to protect her from any flying debris.

The police came storming in surrounding them. He turned over his gun and showed them his badge. Blake started crying, and he led her outside where she was swallowed up by Wendy and the emergency medical team. Ethan and Brian Newsome were standing in the street waiting for him.

"That was pretty damn stupid!" Brian said as Logan approached, a uniformed officer following behind him.

Logan looked at Ethan, he was wearing his poker face, but Logan could tell by the muscles in Ethan's neck and jaw that he was angry. Logan looked back at Brian. "Maybe."

"We need to debrief."

Logan nodded, "Okay,"

"Detective Newsome, here's his weapon." The uniformed officer held up an evidence bag with Logan's gun in it.

Brian frowned but accepted it. "Thanks. Logan come with me."

"You plan on charging him?" Ethan asked.

"No, we just need to work out what happened inside."

Ethan nodded. "We'll talk later," He said to Logan.

Logan nodded and followed Brian to his car. He expected there was going to be hell to pay with Ethan back at the office. What he had done wasn't that different from what had happened on the pier with Jared, no, this was worse. Logan looked around, trying to find Blake in the crowd. They made eye contact before he ducked into the unmarked police car.

Two hours later, Logan walked into the office to find Ethan waiting for him. He steadied his breathing and stood in the middle of the room, waiting.

Ethan looked up and leaned back in his chair. "That didn't take long."

"No, they weren't happy, but Brian said there wasn't much they could do about it."

"That is generous because they could file a complaint."

Logan looked contrite. "It is,"

Ethan shook his head and then stood up. "What the hell were you thinking?"

"I...,"

"Stop! You weren't thinking, or rather were thinking about the wrong thing. If you wanted to charge in there that is fine, but you do it the right way, you talk to me, we organize something."

"Ethan...,"

"No, you don't get to talk." Ethan came to stand in Logan's face. Logan had a couple of inches on him and about twenty pounds. "You acted recklessly and put my best agent at risk unnecessarily. It was just flat out stupid!" Ethan's temper was getting the better of him and he stepped away from Logan. "You didn't even wear a vest, you big dumb ass!"

Logan knew there was nothing he could say, Ethan was completely right, if the roles were reversed, he would tell Ethan the same thing.

"Just because you have a thing for this girl, doesn't mean you are no longer part of this team, unless you don't want to be!"

Logan stared at Ethan, "I am part of the team,"

"Well, good I'm glad to freaking hear it. I just don't get it man, everything you did was wrong, and you do understand that, right? You're supposed to mentoring Jared. Didn't we just have this talk a week ago?"

"Yes,"

"I thought so, clearly you weren't listening then, are you listening now?"

"Yes,"

"Are you sure, because I'm not so sure." Ethan suddenly looked tired.

"Ethan...,"

Ethan raised his hand to stop Logan, "I have to write this up, you get that, right? I don't want to, but I don't have a choice."

Logan had been expecting this, and he appreciated that it was justified. He had put Ethan in a very bad situation with the risks he had taken today.

Ethan sighed. "You're suspended for three days, go home and make sure you heard me this time."

Logan stared at the floor. There was no point in arguing. What could he say? "Okay, Ethan."

"Is Blake okay?"

Ethan saw the pain cross Logan's face.

"I don't know, boss. She hasn't answered my text messages."

"Give her some space. It was pretty traumatic for her today."

Logan nodded and turned to leave.

CHAPTER FIFTEEN

Logan drove to his cottage; the air was thick with fog when he got out of the truck and walked around the back of the house. He had screwed up; he had let down his team; and risked his life to save Blake. Now Blake wasn't even talking to him. What had he expected? He shot her ex-husband right in front of her. That had to be traumatic, even if she and Jerry were no longer together. She had been stalked and held at gunpoint. And what did he do? Come in with guns blazing and kill her ex. Very smooth. He unlocked the back door and grabbed a beer out of the fridge. His phone chirped an incoming call.

He cracked open a beer and answered it.

"Yeah?"

"Logan?" Blake's voice had never sounded so sweet to him.

"Blake, are you okay?"

"Physically, yeah. Just a little shook up. They gave me something to help me sleep at the hospital, but I wanted to call you before I took it."

"Blake, look, I'm really sorry about the way things ended. I feel bad about what happened."

There was a long pause. He wondered if she had hung up.

"You did what you had to do, I'm not sure it could not have ended any other way."

Logan breathed a sigh of relief. He was afraid she would hate him for what he did.

"How are you?" she asked.

"I'm fine."

"I saw you getting into that car, what happened? Did you get in trouble?"

"Nothing you need to worry about."

"Logan, is that how friends treat each other? Keeping secrets?"

He noticed she used the word friends, and that stung. "I got suspended for three days and Ethan wrote me up."

"Why?"

"Because I didn't come in there to rescue you with permission. I acted alone, and that is a dangerous thing. No one knew I was in there, and I actually could have made the situation worse. I wasn't wearing my vest and I could have gotten all of us killed."

"I don't see it like that."

"I'm glad, because I didn't see it that way at the time either. All I could think about was getting you out of there safely."

"Thank you."

He nodded, knowing she couldn't see him.

"Logan, I think I'm going to need some time to process all of this."

He didn't blame her. "Okay,"

"I'll call you soon."

"Okay."

"Thank you, again."

"Sure."

There was another pause and then the phone went dead in his hand. She was gone. He threw the phone across the room and watched it explode against the refrigerator. He walked outside with his beer well so much for making plans for Valentine's Day. There were enough chocolate and flowers to make up for killing her ex-husband.

***

Blake stared at the phone for a few minutes. Then looked over at Wendy.

"He got in trouble for today."

Wendy frowned. "He did it for you, I'm sure he wasn't thinking about proper procedure today."

"I am aware of that," Blake sighed. "Logan is a great guy, and I should be swept off my feet by him, literally coming in and saving me,"

"But...," Wendy looked at her, waiting for more.

"I am afraid to tie myself to another person so tightly again. It didn't end well the last time."

Wendy came over and sat next to Blake on the floral print sofa, "None of this is your fault. None of it! You did everything right."

"Then why do I feel so awful?"

"Because even when you do everything right, things can still go badly." Wendy put an arm around Blake's shoulder and gave her a little squeeze, "Now, take the medicine and get some sleep. I'll stay with you."

Blake nodded and did as she was told.

***

"Logan, are you here?" Kay called out as she walked into Logan's cottage. She saw the pieces of the cell phone lying about on the floor. She stooped down and gathered them up and laid them on the table. It clearly couldn't be fixed, but she couldn't bring herself to just throw it away. "Logan?" She noticed the trash can in the corner had a few beer bottles and a pizza box shoved in it picking it up, she took it outside to the garbage bin and dumped it. No sign of Logan outside. She walked back inside and walked into the living room. She saw a large foot hanging over the arm of the sofa, then an arm over the back. Logan was face down in a pair of sweatpants and no shirt. She had to admit, as much as she loved Ethan, Logan was a good-looking man. Women fell over themselves for him, but he was never interested. He wasn't a one-night stand sort of guy, and he found no one he cared enough about to spend time with until he met Blake. And now she was breaking his heart. She had to fight the urge to track this Blake down and tell her what a huge mistake she was making.

She stood there trying to decide the best way to wake Logan up. She was afraid if she touched him, he might respond without looking first, there was a real possibility that she could end up on the floor. Instead, she crept back into the kitchen and found what she needed to make coffee. She sat at his kitchen table sipping a cup when until he finally stumbled into the kitchen.

He froze as soon as he saw her, "Geeze, Kay!" He put his hand over his heart, "You nearly gave me a heart attack."

"Sorry,"

"What are you doing here?"

"Just enjoying the view and drinking your coffee," she smiled.

"Humph." He shuffled to the cabinet for a coffee mug and poured a cup. He took a sip before joining her at the table.

He sat down with a thud in the chair and drank some more coffee. Finally, he seemed to find his words. "Ethan, send you?"

"No, he doesn't even know I'm here."

"Great, listen if you don't mind can you text him and tell him where you are, I'm in enough trouble without him thinking I'm making time with his girl."

"So, I hear."

"Yeah?"

"He tell you I screwed up?"

"Eventually, he did. But mostly he was pretty upset with himself and Logan, he really didn't enjoy having to do what he did."

Logan sighed, "I know he didn't I shouldn't have put him in that situation."

She nodded; she would not push him to talk. But when Ethan had come home so angry and upset, she felt like she needed to check on Logan. The two of them had never been at odds before. Even when Ethan was the one screwing up, Logan bailed him out. Now Ethan felt compelled to do the same. But the rules were different when you were the boss, not just the friend. Kay understood that more than anyone.

Logan drained his mug, "I'm going to go take a shower, can you hang around a while?"

"Sure." She nodded.

She got up and poured another cup of coffee and took it outside onto the deck to enjoy the view.

She heard the door open and close behind her. Logan came to stand next to her. "I don't understand what's wrong with me."

Kay turned to face him, "The last time we talked, you were telling me how much you care about Blake, has anything changed?"

"Not really."

"Are you sure?"

"I'm not sure what she wants. We were getting along, just hanging out. I didn't even ask for a kiss, even though I wanted to kiss her more than anything. But I was respecting her space. But then her ex shows up and starts stalking her. She called me when he was outside of her apartment, but then wouldn't let me in or even talk to me afterwards. She got freaked out because she found out I shot someone, then he kidnaps her and I rescue her, but I had to kill him to do it. So now she doesn't want to see me. What am I supposed to do?"

"Let me ask you something, did she ask you to be her knight in shining armor?"

"Well, I'd say yes, in a way when she called me when Jerry was outside her apartment."

Kay nodded. "Maybe she was just calling a friend, the one person she knew that would come and help her."

Logan looked like he was contemplating her words.

"So, you're saying that she means more to me than I mean to her."

"I can't answer that question. What I am saying is that you need to make sure you aren't seeing something that isn't there. That you are projecting your feelings onto her."

"I hear what you're saying Kay, but I have never felt like this about anyone before."

"I get that, but it doesn't mean she's the one."

Logan looked sad and stared out over the marsh.

"I really came here to tell you how bad Ethan feels about all of this and he wouldn't say it, and he is hoping you can forgive him."

"He is doing his job, I'm the one who put him in this position. He has nothing to worry about. It should be me hoping he forgives me for acting like an ass and putting the investigation at risk.

She patted him on the shoulder and gave him a kiss on the cheek. "If this girl is the one for you, then I'm happy for you, but if not then I can't promise I won't scratch her eyes out for making you feel like this."

Logan smiled at Kay, "I sure wish you had a sister."

Kay threw her head back and laughed. "God, can you imagine if there were two of us. Just remember if you don't love yourself, how do you expect anyone else to love you."

"You love me, though." He smiled.

"I always will." She squeezed his shoulder and left.

CHAPTER SIXTEEN

Logan drove downtown to buy a new cell phone on his way to the office. He had to admit it was nice not having a phone for a couple of days.

He walked into the office, and everyone was in their places, working hard. He looked over at his desk and his chest tightened.

"Ethan, a word?" He said as he walked straight to the conference room. He needed to talk to Ethan before he faced the others.

Ethan rose slowly and followed Logan, closing the door behind him.

"I've tried calling you twice." Ethan said to Logan's back.

"Yeah, I dropped my cell phone and just got a replacement this morning." Logan turned to face him.

Ethan nodded. Logan was sure that Kay had told him about finding his cell phone busted on the floor. "Listen, I realize I've been doing this a lot lately, and it gets old. But I want to apologize for everything. I shouldn't have put you in such an awkward position and it was selfish to have gone in there after Blake on my own and it was stupid. I knew it even as I did it, but I just had to do it."

Ethan stood quietly until Logan was finished.

Logan ran his hand through his blond curly hair. He needed a haircut. "I don't know what has gotten into me lately, but I want you to know I used these past several days to get my head on straight and I will not let you or the team down again."

Ethan just nodded; he had a sense Logan wasn't done yet.

"Ethan, are we good?" Logan looked as if he was pleading and Ethan couldn't take it.

"Of course, we're good." He reached out and gave Logan a quick hug and slap on the back.

"Yeah?" Logan looked at Ethan, trying to read his face.

"Yeah man, it's all good."

Logan seemed to accept Ethan at his word and smiled. "Okay."

"Alright, let's get some work done." Ethan said smiling.

"You got it, boss.

***

After a week off, Blake returned to the bookstore. The Dean of the College of Engineering and Architecture had called her to ask her to take over a class after a professor had been injured in a car accident. It was mid-semester and Blake had spent the past couple of days preparing to take over the class. She promised Wendy one last full week of work before she had to cut her hours back to accommodate her new teaching schedule.

She was grateful that she was the first one to the store; she hadn't been back since Logan had shot and killed Jerry there. Wendy had done a magnificent job cleaning. The blood that had pooled on the floor from Jerry's head was gone. It was as if Wendy had erased the entire scenario. Blake stood staring at the spot where Jerry died for several long minutes before going to stand where Logan had been when he pulled the trigger. She had spent the last week trying to decide how she felt about all of it and of course, would never had wished to see Jerry hurt, much less killed, but she understood why Logan had shot him. Something had happened to Jerry, and he had changed more than she realized. He had pointed a gun at her, at Wendy, and ultimately at Logan, and that was his mistake. Logan was trained to shoot, to kill in such situations. Blake had known how it would end as soon as she saw Logan peering around the bookshelf. Logan would protect her no matter what, and she knew he had killed people before, so she knew he wouldn't hesitate if he thought she was in eminent danger. She was also relieved that she didn't have to look over her shoulder anymore. She heard the back door open, and she moved back towards the counter so that no one would see her standing there staring.

Wendy called out. "Anyone here?"

"I'm here, up front."

"Oh Blake, how are you today?" Wendy asked, even though she had talked to Blake every day.

"I'm fine, ready to move on."

Wendy looked at her with concern but said nothing. "Okay then, let's get to work. I want to change the displays for the spring."

"Okay, do you want something for St. Patrick's Day, something school related or just spring?"

"Hmm, in honor of your new teaching job let's do something school related. How about we have a science and math display and a creative arts display, try to make the groupings broad?"

Blake nodded. "Okay, I'll start with science and math."

Wendy nodded. "I'll do the arts,"

They got to work carrying armloads of books to displace tables and finding odd bits of art from around the store to enhance the displays. By lunch time, they were both ready for a break.

"Want to have something delivered?"

"Sure, what are you hungry for?"

"Pizza or Chinese?"

"Pizza."

Wendy nodded and grabbed the phone. "A girl after my own heart."

While Wendy was on the phone a customer came in, Blake moved towards the counter and watched the tall good-looking man about her age. He gravitated to the science and math display.

"Can I help you find anything?" She offered.

He looked up, surprised, as if he hadn't realized she was even there. "No, I'm just getting ideas for my students."

"Oh, you're a teacher?"

One corner of his mouth raised just slightly, "I teach at Batten University."

"Oh, I will be teaching there in another week. I'll be taking over for Professor Denton." Blake offered and wondered why she had said such a thing to a complete stranger.

"What subject?"

"Architecture."

His demeanor changed, and he looked at her with something akin to respect. "Which classes?"

"Undergraduate level classes, Design Studio and Architectural Design."

"How many days," he asked, slipping into a comfortable conversation.

"Monday's Wednesdays, and Fridays."

"So, if I may ask what you are doing working here?"

"Well, I just moved here this winter, and I needed something to do until school started."

He nodded either his approval or understanding; she wasn't sure which. "Oh, I'm Simon." He held out his hand.

She shook his hand, "Blake,"

"It is a pleasure to meet you, Blake." He smiled a whole smile this time, and she noticed he had perfectly straight teeth, that seemed to fit him just like everything else about him.

"What do you teach?"

"Civil Engineering, so we will be in the same building."

Blake couldn't stop the smile that was creeping across her face. "Well, then I'm sure I'll see you, again."

"Yeah, I'm sure you will." He smiled and left. Blake stood watching him through the window.

A small cough caught her attention. She turned to see Wendy starting at her.

"What?" Blake asked.

"I'd kill to have your problems, you know that?"

"What?"

"First, Logan and now Simon?"

"Oh, it isn't like that."

"Not to you, but have you ever stopped to ask yourself what it is like for them?"

"No," she said in a small voice.

"I thought you liked Logan."

"I do, of course, I do."

"The way you were looking at Simon, made me think you had forgotten Logan."

"He teaches at the university too; it would be nice to have a friend my first day."

"Really? To do what, walk you to class?" Wendy raised a skeptical eyebrow.

"I can appreciate more than one good looking man, can't I?"

"Sure, you can, but just be careful which hearts you break."

"What do you mean?"

"Girl, Logan has some powerful feelings for you and I really would hate to see him get his heart broken, if you're not sure about him, please don't string him a long."

Blake could feel her face heat up to the point she had to turn away from Wendy's scrutiny. She did care for Logan a lot. He was so intense, and lately it made her a little uncertain of their relationship, such as it was. They hadn't spent any time together after the day of fishing and kayaking at his river cottage. After things had gotten a little crazy with Jerry stalking her. Simon wasn't part of all that, it felt good to talk to him. She didn't think he shot people regularly and didn't know her past. It was like she was starting over with him. Logan had saved her from her past, but now he was also a reminder.

"We had one date, Wendy. I don't think he is ready for a commitment just yet." She tried to dismiss Wendy's concerns.

Wendy gave her a look that said she wasn't buying it, but she didn't say any more. She let Blake consider her own feelings.

CHAPTER SEVENTEEN

"How you are doing, Logan?" Kay asked as she walked into the FBI office.

Logan looked up from his computer, "Fine, you looking for Ethan?"

"I am."

"He's in the conference room. He should be out in a minute."

"Okay, thanks." Kay smiled. "Have you talked to Blake lately?"

"A week ago, she's busy grading papers and stuff." Logan looked like his eyes were about to glass over at the very thought.

"I see. You talked to her on the phone. But when was the last time you spent time with her?"

Logan leaned back in his chair, frustration showing on his face. That look no longer phased Kay. She waited patiently for him to answer.

"It's been a while."

"Why don't you ask her out to dinner or something. You guys could come over and have dinner at our place." She smiled sweetly.

Logan's brow knitted together. "I don't think she wants to see me."

"Have you asked to see her?"

"Well, no. It's just a feeling."

"I see," Kay said as she watched Ethan walk out of the conference room and over to her, "You won't know unless you ask." Kay smiled before leaning in for a kiss on the cheek from him.

Logan watched the two of them with a stabbing pain in his chest. Logan stood up, "Jared, let's go hit the range."

Jared looked up, pretending he hadn't heard the exchange between Logan and Kay. "Okay."

Kay watched the two men leave.

"How's he doing?" She whispered to Ethan.

Ethan nodded towards the kitchen to take their conversation out of earshot of other people in the office.

"He's laser focused on his work and trying really hard with Jared."

Kay nodded, "in other words he's a mess."

Ethan smiled and nodded. "Pretty much."

"I wish he would just call her and ask her out. It seems they are both just dancing around each other."

"I think we both need to stay out of it." Ethan tried to end the discussion.

"Hmmmm," Kay muttered, which meant she heard what Ethan was saying and didn't agree with him at all.

***

"Hi Blake, how's classes going?"

Blake looked up to see Simon standing in the classroom's doorway.

"Well, at least I got over the jitters." She smiled.

"Wanna walk over to the student center and grab a coffee?" He tilted his head to the side.

"Uh," Blake hesitated she had thoughts of going home and relaxing in the tub with a bottle of wine. "Sure, why not?" The tub could wait. She put her notes and laptop into her bag and walked with Simon across the manicured quad lined with dogwoods. There was a large fountain in the center that seemed to be the meeting spot for students waiting to soak up as much of the day's sun as possible in between classes. The student center was an expansive two-story building with two food courts and several small shops offering everything from books and school supplies to electronics for students and instructors alike. They stopped at a popular coffee vendor and waited in line.

Blake felt a little awkward with the lull in their conversation. She was at a loss for topics of conversation. Finally, she found the courage to speak up.

"How is your semester going?"

He smiled sweetly down at her.

"Well, not bad. Lots of eager beavers and some of them won't make it through the add/drop period."

"Really? Why?"

"It is always that way, you'll lose some too." Seeing the look on her face he held up his hands. "It is no reflection on your teaching. Students have big plans to get as much of their required classes done quickly, so they can get to the 'good' stuff and find they have signed up for more classes than they can handle. So, they drop a few. Don't worry, they will be back."

It was their turn to order, and a young girl wearing a ball cap with the coffee vendor logo greeted them. "What can I get you today?"

Simon looked at Blake, "do you like flavored coffees? They have the best."

The barista beamed at Simon.

"I'll have a Caramel Frappuccino." Blake said.

"Excellent choice, I'll have a double espresso room for cream."

"That will be $9.48."

"I've got it," Simon said to Blake, waiving a card over the pad on the counter.

"Oh, thanks."

They moved to the side and waited for their order. Blake looked around, amazed by the number of people. The campus was like its own city with transportation via shuttle buses, shops, restaurants, the dorms and apartments. It was impressive. And just like any other city, there were employees who commuted in and out.

They got their drinks and Simon motioned to a seating area where they grabbed seats and a small table for two. Blake looked around, watching the ebb and flow of students and faculty.

"Wow, this place is really busy."

Simon looked around as if noticing the crowd of people for the first time. "Yeah, this is a sort of the central hub of everything."

"How long have you taught here?"

"Six years, I'm up for tenure this year."

"Oh, that's exciting!"

"Yeah, I guess. It's a little stressful."

"I can imagine. I'm sure you won't have any problems though." She wanted to sound supportive, she actually had no idea what was required for tenure. The school had sent her literature when she was hired, but she hadn't paid too much attention to that part since she was only a part-time instructor, it hadn't seemed relevant.

"Is there a lot of competition for tenure?"

"There are a couple of us this year that are eligible. I used to think I wanted it more than anything, now that it is here, I'm not so sure."

"What will you do?"

"I'll try for it, but if I don't get it, I won't be as disappointed as I might have been at one time."

She wondered what could have made him so cynical in just six years of teaching. She wanted to ask but held back.

"Well, I hope you get it if it brings you happiness." She said honestly.

He looked at her curiously and smiled. "Thank you."

She nodded and sipped her coffee. When they were done, he stood up, "I hate to leave you, but I have office hours in ten minutes, and I need to get going."

"Oh, okay. Well, thank you for the coffee and the company." She smiled.

"Anytime." He waved and disappeared into the throng of students leaving the building.

She sat for a minute watching the crowd. It was nearly seven before she finally made it home, and she found she was exhausted. She kicked off her shoes and ran some bath water. She thought about sending Logan a text message just to say hi, but then decided against it; instead, she put the phone on the charger and poured herself a glass of wine.

CHAPTER NINETEEN

Blake rushed into Bumboat Books, pulling the door closed quickly behind her. "Morning!" Unwrapping her scarf from her neck and shed her coat as she walked towards the back of the store to hang them up. "Is it ever going to warm up?"

Wendy popped her head out from the Suspense and Mystery aisle, "Morning!"

"Sure, June is lovely here." Wendy laughed.

"Really?" Blake came to stand at the end of the aisle where Wendy was shelving new books.

"Are you kidding me, how is that we got more snow in the valley and it never felt this cold?"

"The water makes a difference, it is cold and damp, plus here we don't ease into it, it's hot one day, freezing the next, it doesn't allow the body to adjust."

"The kids at school don't seem to notice they are wearing shorts and flip-flops!"

Wendy laughed, "yeah that sounds about right."

Blake shook her head, "What can I do to help this morning?"

"I need a new display."

"On it!"

"How's school going?"

"Oh, pretty good, there is a lot more to it than I realized, but I am enjoying it."

Wendy smiled she was glad that Blake seemed to have been able to put her past behind her and get on with her new life.

"Heard from Logan lately?"

"Yeah, he left me a message last night asking me out. I haven't called him back yet."

"Blake, you need to decide how you feel about Logan. And if needs be, let him go."

Blake sighed. She was all too aware of her feelings for Logan. "I know how I feel about him that's the problem."

"How is that a problem?" Wendy asking, coming around to face Blake.

"The problem is my feelings about him scare me."

Wendy looked at her puzzled, "You're afraid of Logan?"

Blake put down the stack of books she was arranging.

"No, I'm not afraid of Logan, although I sure wouldn't want to be on his bad side, but what scares me about Logan is me. I don't want to make the same mistake twice and it is just so easy to give myself over to him and not look back."

"And how is that a bad thing? Just because one man took advantage of your emotions and your devotion doesn't mean another man will."

Blake hesitated, she was afraid to speak the words out loud, as if they would be even more terrifying once they were loose in the world.

"My heart just wants to explode every time I look at him. And when he isn't around, there is a huge aching hole in the middle of my chest. I can't imagine my life without him."

Wendy looked at her and waited.

"I could so easily give my life over to him, heart, body and soul. Look what happened the last time I did that." A single tear escaped down her cheek.

Wendy came to wrap her arms around her. "Child, there is nothing wrong with leading with your heart the way you do. Logan is not Jerry. You understand that. I didn't know Jerry, but it is clear he didn't really love you. Imagine if Logan feels the same way about you? What if Logan would give his heart, body and soul to you? What if his heart wants to explode because it is filled with so much love?"

Blake looked at Wendy and blinked. "Do you think that is how he feels about me?"

"I can't tell you that, Logan is the only one who can answer that question." Wendy smiled and focused on a stack of books.

Blake stood for a long moment staring at the table with the books and decorations strewn about. Then she took out her phone and sent Logan a text.

"Hi, sorry I missed your call last night."

She waited, and when she didn't get an immediate reply; she pocketed the phone. She had less enthusiasm than she had before. Wendy kept an eye on her through the gaps in the books. She hoped Blake would come to her senses.

An hour later the display was done, Blake stood admiring her handy work and not being fully satisfied with it. Wendy was at the counter helping a customer when the door to the shop opened and the cold air swept in. Blake shivered and looked up.

Logan filled the entire doorway; he closed the door, scanning the room. He spotted her and her heart leapt into her throat. Just like it did every time his eyes met hers.

Logan had to step out of the way to let a customer leave moving towards Blake.

"I got your text." He said quietly.

"I got your message." She said stupidly.

"Yeah, sorry it was so late, I didn't realize the time...,"

Blake shook her head. "It's okay, its not late, I was just in the middle of something. I'm sorry I should have called you back when I was done." She lied she didn't want to tell him that she was soaking in a hot bath with a bottle of wine and thinking about him.

"Don't worry about it."

Blake could see it in his eyes that he knew she was lying. She should have known better. He was an FBI agent, for god's sake; they trained him to tell when people were lying. She admonished herself.

"I'm glad you're here now, though." She tried to move past her indiscretion.

Logan smiled a big goofy smile that made her giggle.

"I'm going to have a little crab boil at the cottage tonight with Ethan and the team. You want to come?"

"It sounds like a work thing,"

"No, they are all bring guests, you wouldn't be out of place."

"You sure?"

"Of course."

"Yeah, that sounds like fun." And she meant it.

"Great, what time do you get off work?"

"Five,"

"Perfect, can I pick you up?"

"Yes," she nodded. It was a big step for her to not take her own car and have a means to leave when she was ready. She trusted Logan, and having lived here for several months now, she wasn't so helpless.

Logan smiled at her again, and she felt it all the way into her soul.

"Okay, well, I've gotta run and pick up a few things, I'll see you later."

She nodded.

"The display looks great by the way." He grinned and left.

Blake looked down at the table she had forgotten all about it.

Wendy looked at her and smiled.

The day seemed to drag, Blake thought five o'clock would never get there. When Wendy switched the sign around to read "closed", Logan knocked on the door.

"Oh, hey Logan, come on in." Wendy reopened the door. "Blake, Logan is here!" She called out.

Blake appeared, holding her coat and wrapping her scarf around her neck. Logan tried to suppress a smile.

"What?"

"You look like you're ready for the arctic circle." He grinned.

"Please tell me you're wearing thermals under that sweatshirt?"

Logan grinned, "Nope." He said lifting his sweatshirt slightly revealing his flat abdomen. It was all Blake could do to keep from ogling.

Wendy suppressed a giggle.

"Here, let me help you with your coat." Logan walked over and took the green wool coat from her and held it.

"Thank you."

"You kids have fun!" Wendy said as she stepped out the back door.

"Why don't you come too," Logan offered.

"Oh, I wish I could, but I've got exciting plans tonight."

"Really?" Blake was surprised Wendy had said nothing earlier about going out.

"Yeah, I'm going to a lecture on medieval art."

Blake looked at her as if she were joking.

"I'm serious. The fine arts gallery is sponsoring a lecture series this month."

Logan looked at Blake, "Would you rather go to that? It sounds infinitely more fascinating."

Wendy swatted him, "You hush up Logan Watson!"

Logan laughed and steered Blake through the employee's back entrance.

Blake sat quietly, watching the sunset as they drove out of the city to Logan's cottage.

"Everything okay?"

Blake refocused on Logan and smiled. "Yes, I was just thinking about how beautiful the sunset is tonight."

"Storms coming."

"How can you tell?"

"The clouds, they make for a beautiful sunset but also means a storm will blow in off the water next day or so."

"Really?"

"Trust me." He grinned.

'Trust me', those words brought back the memory of Logan rescuing her from Jerry. Logan had asked her to trust him, and she did. He had saved her life.

"I trust you more than anyone."

Logan caught the seriousness of her tone and looked at her. "Everything okay?"

"Yeah." She nodded. "Perfect."

Logan nodded and returned his gaze to the road ahead.

"Since I didn't prepare anything to bring with me to your crab boil, can I help you cook or something?"

"Nope, already taken care of." He smiled as he pulled into the driveway. Blake was surprised to see everyone else was there already. She gave him a questioning look.

"It takes a long time to prep and cook. Ethan and I started early." He grinned.

Suddenly she was very nervous.

"Everything alright?"

"I think I am the odd man out."

"You think that now, but once you go inside and start talking to everyone, you will feel right at home."

"I hope you're right."

"I'll make you a deal, if after an hour you're still uncomfortable and want to leave, I'll take you home. No questions asked. Deal?"

She nodded, "Deal."

"Okay, let's go." Logan came around and opened her door for her and together they walked around the house to the deck.

Everyone on the deck cheered when they saw them.

"Hey, there you two are. We were getting worried." Ethan called out.

"Yeah, we thought Blake had decided to hang out with a better class of people." Jared laughed.

Blake blushed as she thought about the hanging out with Simon on campus. She had to remember that these people could read her without even realizing it. She tensed for a moment. Logan squeezed her hand and whispered in her ear.

"Trust me."

She gave him a weak smile and nodded.

A woman she didn't recognize stepped forward. Everything about her oozed confidence.

"Don't listen to them Blake," the woman held out her hand. "I'm Kay."

"Hello."

"I'm afraid Jared and Ethan started the party without our host and have had a beer or two by now. They are harmless but can be a couple of idiots too." She laughed.

Blake found she was laughing along with her. She couldn't imagine Ethan being an idiot. He was possibly more up tight than Logan. Kay walked over to a cooler.

"Would you like something to drink, there is water and soda, if you don't want beer. And a pitcher of tea in the kitchen."

Blake looked around the deck the firepit down below was roaring with a grate over it. And Logan had two outdoor heaters that looked like the ones used downtown by all the pubs and cafes. No one was wearing a coat, and she looked out of place.

"Perhaps tea."

"Okay, come on." Kay led her into the house and poured her a glass of iced tea. "Do you want me to take your coat?"

"It seems kinda cold out there."

"It is a beautiful coat, why don't we hang it up and find a sweatshirt of Logan's for you to wear. I'd hate for your coat to smell like crabs and beer." Kay smiled.

Blake nodded, "I am wearing a sweater."

"Okay, well we'll try that but if you get cold, we'll find you something, okay?"

"Okay." Blake smiled. She liked Kay already.

Kay and Blake joined everyone at the firepit to check the progress of the dinner. Jared and Stephanie were anchoring down newspaper over a picnic table that hadn't been there the last time Blake had visited Logan's cottage.

"It's just about ready. Grab a seat!" Ethan called out.

Blake and Kay joined them all at the table.

"Do you guys do this often?" Blake asked.

"Not as often as we like, but as often as we can." Jared smiled.

Blake nodded, "is there anything I can do to help?"

"Yeah, eat some of these crabs," Ethan said as he and Logan dumped crab, shrimp, and corn on the cob on the table. "There is more where that came from."

Blake looked up and down the table. Never having been to a crab boil before, she wasn't sure what to do.

Logan sat down next to her and handed her some tools that looked like a nutcracker and a pick.

"Try it like this," He picked up a crab, pulled a leg off of it and gently cracked it open so that the meat inside slid right out. He dipped it in drawn butter and popped it in his mouth.

She copied him but the meat didn't slide out; it was still inside the two halves of the crab leg.

"It's okay, that happens, so you can try cracking a little more with this or use the pick to pull it out gently."

She followed Logan's example. She struggled with the first few, but by her second crab she got the hang of it. Soon, with all the eating and talking, listening to the group tell stories about each other, she forgot how cold it was. She felt right at home with this group. She even lost track of time.

Finally, the food was gone, and everyone was relaxed. They cleaned up and settled in on the deck with drinks under the heaters.

Logan leaned over and whispered, "You okay?"

Blake smiled and nodded. "Yes."

"Good." Logan leaned back, looking pleased with himself. He sat close to her as he resisted the urge to put his arm around her. He didn't want to rush things or crowd her. Logan wasn't sure what she thought about a relationship with him, although he was fairly sure she didn't blame him for the death of her ex-husband.

Blake's phone vibrated in her jeans pocket. She pulled it out to see Simon's name brightly on the screen, and she was sure Logan had seen it. She stared at it, debating whether or not to answer it.

"You going to get that?" Logan asked.

"Um, yeah." She touched the screen, "Hello?"

"Hey, Blake. It's Simon wanted to see if you were up for karaoke tonight with the Engineering crew?"

"Oh thanks, Simon, I appreciate that. I already have plans tonight, maybe some other time."

"Okay, no problem. Next time."

She tapped the screen to end the call and pocketed the phone.

"Everything alright?" Kay asked, knowing Logan wanted to know, but wouldn't ask.

"Yeah, some of the other instructors were going out and were nice enough to invite me along."

"Do you need me to drop you somewhere to meet them?" Logan asked. Blake could hear the distance in his voice.

"No, they aren't really my crowd, and I'm definitely not into karaoke." She tried to laugh. Logan relaxed a little, but not like he was before the phone call.

"You could invite them here," He offered.

"No, like I said, they were just being nice. They are not really my crowd. They are younger, mostly they are really focused on getting tenure."

"That isn't something you would be interested in?" Kay asked, trying to relieve some pressure.

"No," Blake shook her head. "I've enjoy teaching this semester, but honestly. I don't think it is something I would want to do full time. I think I would like to go back to the private sector and get back into design work."

"Really?"

"Yeah, I've been thinking about it as the semester is getting ready to end. Academia is not what I expected, and I really miss designing things."

"You and I will talk later, but I have an idea for you." Kay smiled.

"Ut oh." Ethan said under this breath.

Kay elbowed him in the ribs. Blake laughed at their playfulness. That is what she wanted, a relationship like Kay and Ethan.

"Wanna take a walk?" Logan offered.

"Sure."

They got up and walked to the river; it was dark away from the lights of the house. With the storm that was coming, there were no stars or moon. She looked up at Logan, "Everything alright?"

"Oh yeah. Just fine."

She nodded, though she doubted he could see her.

"You were right."

"About what?" He asked.

"I do feel right at home, your friends are wonderful."

"Good, I'm glad."

She stood listening to the water lap against the banks.

"It is so peaceful here, now that I have lived here a while, I can't imagine living anywhere else. I love the water." She tried to fill the awkward silence.

"Blake, I need to ask you something." Logan's voice was low and she could tell by the tone he had something heavy weighing on his mind.

"Ask me anything."

"I know you've been through a lot and I don't want to push you into something you don't want to do...,"

"Logan, just ask. It's okay."

"May I kiss you? I've been thinking about it all night and it's driving me crazy,"

"Yes,"

"We haven't had a proper date or anything, but I just can't help it."

"Logan, I said, yes."

She could tell he had stopped breathing, and she reached out in search of his hands.

"Kiss me." She whispered.

Logan leaned down and brushed his lips gently against hers like he was afraid to touch her. She tilted her head further back and stepped closer to him.

This time his lips touched her more firmly. They were warm and soft, and her heart and mind were going to explode from his touch. She let his tongue tentatively traced her mouth. Her knees weaken and a small moan involuntarily escaped her lips. Logan cradled her face as her tongue sought his. It was almost more than either of them could bear. Logan wrapped his arms around her and pulled her close. She held on to him while her heart and soul gave themselves over to him.

Finally, Logan took a step back and stared down at her. "Blake Morgan, you are the most incredible woman I have ever met."

Blake wasn't sure what to say. Instead, she gently caressed his face. Logan captured her delicate hand in his and kissed it.

"Blake, I don't know how you feel about me, but I have to tell you something," He waited for her response when she remained silent, he continued. "My heart has been yours since the first time I looked at you and there has been some crazy stuff between, but no matter what happens after tonight. I want you to know there will never be anyone else. My heart is forever yours."

Blake's eyes welled up. It was like a fairytale, Logan was her knight in shining armor, and she couldn't believe that she had ever mistaken what she had with Jerry for genuine love, now that it was standing in front of her in the form of Logan.

She took his hand in both of hers and held it against her heart.

"You have my heart always." She said.

He let out his breath, like he had been holding it. She shivered as a breeze came down the river.

"Come on, let's make you warm." He put his arm around her and led her back towards the house.

When they got there, everyone was gone.

"Where did they all go, oh no! We were rude to them!" She felt embarrassed for leaving his friends.

"Don't be ridiculous we weren't rude, Ethan and Kay come in and out of here whenever they want."

They walked inside to find a note on the table from Kay,

Had to go, see you soon. Tell Blake, I'll call her. Love Kay.

Logan read her the note, "See, everything is alright."

Blake nodded.

"Come on, let's get you warmed up." He led her to the sofa and sat down, then pulled her down in his lap and wrapped his arms around her.

The next morning, they were in the same position when they woke up.

CHAPTER TWENTY

"Hi Blake, missed you this weekend with the gang." Simon caught up to Blake in the hallway after her last class.

"Oh, hey Simon, did you guys have a good time?"

"Yeah, we did. Wish you could have been there."

"Thanks, but Karaoke isn't really my thing." She smiled.

"Well, it was last minute too," Simon said apologetically.

"Yeah, I was already out with some friends when you called."

"Oh."

She noticed the look on Simon's face. She headed for the door.

"Have you heard about your tenure yet?" Blake asked, trying to change the subject and keep it work related.

"Not yet, but soon I hope." They walked down the sidewalk towards the faculty parking. As they got closer, Blake noticed a familiar large pick-up truck and Logan leaning against the hood of her car. She smiled to herself.

"Have you gotten your contract for next semester yet?" Simon asked.

"Not yet," she said, half listening to him now.

He followed her gaze. "Hey why is that guy sitting on your car?"

Before Blake could say more, Simon strode towards Logan.

"Hey buddy, you can't sit on people's cars like that! This is faculty parking only!" Simon pointed towards the pick-up.

Logan never took his eyes off Blake, but he pushed back his blazer just enough for Simon to see the badge hanging there.

"Are you in some sort of trouble?" Simon looked at Blake.

Blake laughed, "No," She walked over to Logan, "Simon, this is Logan. Logan, this is Simon. He is one of the professors I was telling you about."

Logan stood up off the car and held out his hand. "Nice to meet you, Simon. Blake has told me a lot about you."

"A pleasure." Simon smiled stiffly and glanced at Blake.

"Logan took Blake's hand protectively. Sorry to drop in on you like this. We're going to be working late tonight, but I wondered if you had time for a quick bite."

"Yes, I do." Blake smiled at Logan. "Simon, you want to join us. Maybe ask Alesha or Ted to come along?"

"Uh, no thanks, I have office hours this evening. Some other time?"

"Yeah man, that would be great." Logan nodded.

"It was nice meeting you." He turned and walked away.

Blake turned her attention to Logan "Any thoughts for dinner?"

"I was thinking either pizza or burgers, what do you think?"

"Why not go to Capris, we can get both!" She suggested.

"That's why I like you, you think like me." Logan laughed. "I'll meet you there."

"Okay."

Logan moved his truck and followed Blake to the little diner that was between his office and her apartment. It was a cozy, dimly lit family run business where all the tables were booths and the old jukebox had been replaced by a digital version. It wasn't quite the same, but Logan applauded the owner for keeping up with the times. The food was the best in town.

They sat in the corner so that Logan had a view of the door and the dining room.

Blake looked across the table at him and smiled. "That wasn't really fair what you did to Simon."

"What?" Logan played innocent.

"Playing the heavy and flashing your badge." She giggled a little.

"I did him a favor, he was working himself up to make a fool of himself. I just stopped him before it got too far."

Blake laughed.

Logan looked at her seriously for a moment. "You like that guy or what?"

"Yeah, Simon is a nice guy. He came in the bookstore one day and we started talking. I told him I was going to teach a semester at the college, he was nice enough to help me find my way around campus, which I appreciated very much."

Logan nodded. But said nothing else. The server brought their order, a small pizza and a burger with fries to save him from the awkward silence.

Blake steered the subject away from Simon, "You must have a case if you have to work late tonight."

"Yeah, Ethan and I are pulling stake out duty, Jared and Stephanie are there now."

"Anything you can talk about?"

"Well, it isn't classified for anything." He chuckled. "Do you really want to know about the dregs of society?"

"No, I guess not. I want you to tell me how your day was and be there for you if you need to talk about it."

Logan looked at her in surprise. He nodded slowly. "Okay."

"We think we have a lead on the location of a man wanted for human trafficking in Washington."

"That is awful, does he traffic in women or children?"

"Both, although teenage boys are his specialty."

"Oh god," Blake said, "The things you must see in your job." She shook her head in amazement.

"Yeah, some days it is pretty bad, but then it gives you some satisfaction when you can make sure someone is put behind bars."

"What about when you have to shoot someone like that? Do you get the same sense of satisfaction?" She thought perhaps it would be greater since then you would know the monster wouldn't get out of jail.

"No, I don't. I value human life; I never take satisfaction in having to kill another human."

Blake sat there staring at him for a moment. Thinking how quickly the mood of the evening had changed. She wanted to reach out and hug him. To reassure him that he wasn't alone.

"I'm always here for you." She whispered.

"Thank you."

CHAPTER TWENTY-ONE

Blake didn't see Logan over the next few days. He would send a text when he could, but he was busy working on the human trafficking case and she had the end of the semester papers to grade. She had been looking for jobs in the private sector with architectural firms, but so far nothing had panned out.

She was sitting in her office waiting for the next student, when her cell phone rang. It wasn't a number she recognized.

"Hello?"

"Blake, it's Kay."

"Hi, Kay."

"Am I calling at a bad time?"

"No, not at all."

"Listen, I have a job opportunity for you if you're still looking. It is within my company. Do you think we can sit down and talk about it tomorrow?"

"Yeah, I mean yes, of course."

"Okay, what's a good time for you?"

"I'm flexible, I don't have to teach tomorrow."

"Okay, well if it is alright, I will send a car for you. The parking around here can be a pain in the neck sometimes."

"A car?"

"Yeah, a perk of being the CEO, frankly I don't use it often, this will give my driver a chance to earn his paycheck." She laughed.

"Okay, sure. I'll be ready."

"Okay, one o'clock then?"

"One o'clock."

She hung up and thought about the possibilities. She remembered Logan telling her that Kay owned a company that manufactured various engine parts, but she didn't know what that meant. Blake opened her laptop and searched Port City Industries. She was surprised to see how large the company actually was. There were locations in three cities. The headquarters being in Gates Point. They owned a large building across the river from downtown. She spent the next hour finding out what she could online, to help prepare her for the meeting tomorrow. After the office hours were officially over, she was prepared to go home and make sure her portfolio was in order to show Kay.

"Excuse me, Blake,"

Blake looked up to see the chair of the department Dr. Gupta standing in her doorway.

"I really need to know if you plan on teaching next semester. I have a deadline to meet."

"Yes sir, I appreciate your patience," Blake had been putting off answering the request to teach next semester. She enjoyed the students, but this wasn't really the place she pictured herself. She took a chance. "No, I'm afraid I won't be returning next semester."

"I'm very sorry to hear that."

"I appreciate the opportunity but, I don't think teaching is for me. I miss designing."

"I understand." He held out his hand. "You are always welcome to come back if you change your mind."

"Thank you."

After Dr. Gupta left, it was like someone had lifted a weight off her shoulders. She really hoped things worked out with Kay tomorrow. She could always get more hours at the bookstore and in the short-term money wasn't an issue. After Jerry's death, she had received a large payout from his life insurance policy. While she didn't like the idea of spending the money, at least it was there if she needed it.

The next day she pulled one of her suits from the back of the closet. Gathered her portfolio and her laptop. Promptly at one o'clock there was a knock at the door.

"Ms. Morgan? My name is Eddie Green, I'll be taking you to meet Kay Dandridge."

"Nice to meet you, Mr. Green."

"Please call me Eddie," He gave her a charming smile.

"Okay, if you call me Blake."

He nodded and stepped aside to allow her to walk through the door. He opened the car door for her. She settled into the back seat. The interior of was a buttery soft leather. Eddie kept the divider between the front and rear seats open. Blake watched as they drove across town and crossed the river. The buildings became taller and newer, more modern in design. The traffic was heavier over here, and Blake now appreciated Kay sending Eddie to come and get her. It would have taken her forever to navigate her way to the building. Eddie deftly slipped in and out of traffic and into an underground parking garage. He pulled into a reserved spot and opened the door for her once again. She followed him to a heavy metal door that led to a small elevator lobby with an office directory. Port City Industries had the upper floors, and the rest of the building was occupied by a variety of financial and legal firms, a few insurance companies, and some she couldn't determine by the name what type of firm they were. When the elevator car arrived, Eddie pressed the button for the twenty-fifth floor. There was the obligatory music. Finally, the car stopped, and the doors opened.

"Here you go ma'am; Sherry will buzz me when you are ready to leave." Eddie said, clearly not getting off the elevator with her.

"Thank you very much, Eddie." She gave him a sweet smile.

"See you soon." He winked at her. "Just go right through those doors." He pointed to a set of heavy oak unmarked doors.

Blake went through the doors to find another short hallway. At the end she could see an enormous desk.

"Hello, my name is Blake Morgan..."

"Yes, ma'am, Ms. Dandridge is expecting you. Go right in." She nodded to another set of doors.

Blake peeked inside. Kay was sitting behind her desk. She looked up when the door opened.

"Blake!" She rose and came around the desk to greet her.

"Hi, Kay." Blake smiled and felt a little nervous.

"I'm so glad you could come, please have a seat." To Blake's surprise, Kay led her to the conference table and not to the guest chairs at her desk.

"Thank you for having me."

Kay looked at her in surprise. "Are you nervous?"

"Yeah, a little."

Kay gave her a warm smile. "Don't be. Just remember you've seen me elbow deep in crabs and beer."

Blake had to laugh. "I guess you have a point."

"Sit down and relax, can I get you anything to drink?"

"Water?"

Kay walked over to a credenza and opened a door that revealed a mini fridge and pulled out a bottle of water.

"So, I wanted to talk to you about a position I have in the company," Kay sat down next to Blake.

"Okay,"

"My grandfather and father started this company. We have offices in three cities,"

"Yes, I have to admit, I did a little research online."

Kay smiled. "Good. I don't think these offices have been updated in years and I need an architect that can help with space planning and design. I am thinking of moving our office in Connecticut."

"I can certainly help with that. I brought a copy of my portfolio."

"Great, let's take a look." Kay scooted her chair closer.

They spent an hour looking over the designs and drawings from Blake's previous work.

"This is all very impressive." Kay smiled. "So, would you be interested in adding some designs to that portfolio?"

Blake nodded, "I would, but I have a few questions."

Kay sat back and smiled. "Sure,"

"How permanent is this job? I mean a few months, a year?"

"Oh, I imagine much longer than that. I'd want you to manage the construction projects after you design them."

Blake smiled it was like a dream come true.

"I think I can handle that."

"You can start as soon as your teaching job is complete if you like."

Blake smiled again, "That is good, because I told the department Chair yesterday that I wouldn't be teaching next semester."

"Then this is perfect timing."

"Yeah, it is."

"You might have to travel a little, spend some time at the other offices."

"That's okay."

"Okay, good," Kay nodded. "That isn't anything we need to worry about now, because I'd like you to start with these offices first."

"Okay, I'll need to sit down with you and discuss what you have in mind or someone you designate."

"There's just one more thing, you need to sign your employment papers and there is the matter of your salary." Kay got up and walked over to her desk and brought back a folder. She slid it over to Blake.

The letter with a salary was on top. Blake looked at it. And then looked at Kay.

Kay nodded, "is that acceptable?"

"Per year?"

"Yes,"

Blake swallowed hard; she hadn't made this much when she was in the design field in Roanoke.

"Yes, this is acceptable." She tried to keep from smiling. She wanted to maintain her professional demeanor, but she was ecstatic over the salary. That kind of money would allow her freedom she had never had before.

Kay got up once more and pressed a button on her phone. "Sherry, can you join us, please?"

A moment later Sherry, the assistant from out in the hallway came in.

"Sherry can you make copies of all of this paperwork for Blake and then we need to order her some business cards."

"Sure thing." Sherry smiled at Blake and gathered the signed papers. "I'll be back in a moment to take down the information you want on your cards."

Kay smiled, "You okay?"

"It all seems surreal; it is like my life is finally falling into place." She shook her head and smiled.

"Awesome! After Sherry comes back in, I'll show you to your new office, although, you are welcome to work remotely."

"That sounds nice, I'll need to upgrade my laptop for that I'm afraid."

"Don't worry about that, you'll be getting a new laptop anyway, I'll make sure IT puts whatever you need on it. You just tell them, okay? I mean it." Kay had a sense Blake wouldn't want to start making requests for expensive software and equipment. "I need you to do your best if you need anything at all to do that, you will have it understood?"

Blake blinked, "Understood." She had an overwhelming urge to call Logan and tell him the good news. Then she had a terrible thought. "Kay, can I ask you something and please don't be offended."

Kay looked puzzled and sat back. "Questions don't offend me, go ahead."

"This," Blake paused she couldn't believe she was about to ask this question, but she needed to know, "this isn't because of Logan, is it?"

Kay looked at her thoughtfully and smiled. "No, this isn't about Logan. If you and Logan don't stay together, that will have absolutely no bearing on your job here."

Blake studied her for a moment and then decided she believed her. "Okay, then."

Kay nodded, "Okay."

They both smiled. Blake spent two more hours at Port City Industries talking to Kay and Sherry and getting a little orientation as far as benefits and the office procedures. Pretty much you came to Sherry if you needed anything. She would make sure it was handled by one of the other admins or herself.

That evening Logan sent Blake a text, "Up for some company this evening?"

"Yes,"

"I'll drop by around seven."

"See you then."

Logan was on time. Blake breathed a sigh of relief when she saw him.

"Hey," She smiled as she let him in. "Wanna a beer?"

"Yeah, that would be great." Logan followed her to the kitchen.

"How was your day?" She asked.

"Oh well not bad, wrapped up one case started another, you know how it is."

"You arrested the human trafficker?"

"Yes, we did."

"Congratulations! That's great."

Logan lifted one corner of his mouth in a near smile. "Yeah, one down, a zillion more to go."

"You look tired."

"Yeah, I guess I am."

"Come on," She pointed to the sofa, and they sat down.

"I don't want to bore you with the details. How was your day?"

Blake couldn't help but beam at him.

He looked at her curiously, "What?"

"I got a new job today."

Logan sat up straighter, "You did?"

"Yes, private sector. I'll be able to get back into space planning and design."

Logan came alive, "Really? That is great!"

"Yeah, and it pays better than I could have ever imagined."

"Oh Blake, I am so happy for you!" He leaned over and kissed her forehead.

"Thank you, it is like everything is coming together finally."

"That's awesome, we should celebrate."

"Maybe this weekend, when you aren't so tired. Are you hungry?"

"No, not really. Tell me more about this job, what's the name of the company?"

Blake gave him a wicked smile. "Port City Industries."

Logan raised his eyebrows at her, "Kay hired you?"

"Well, you don't have to look so surprised." She swatted at him playfully.

"I don't mean it like that, you are totally qualified, but listen that's huge Kay doesn't hire just anyone. She is very picky about who she hires. That company is her family. She knows all of her employees by name, she knows their kid's names, everything."

"That's good to know."

"Blake, that is really awesome." Logan forgot out tired he was, he was so excited for her.

"Here is one minor catch."

"What's that?"

"I might have to travel a little to her other locations when she is ready to have them remodeled."

"Well, that isn't so bad, is it?" He asked.

"I didn't think so." She grinned. "She said I can work from home when I want."

"I'm so happy for you."

He leaned in again to kiss her, this time he kissed her gently on the mouth. Fire spread through Blake's core. She returned his kiss and ran her hands through his hair. He tasted like beer and Logan. He wrapped his arms around her and held her close; she was leaning into him awkwardly, so he picked her up and put her across his lap while they continued to kiss.

She was lost in his touch. She could not imagine being with anyone else ever again. It was exciting and terrifying at the same time. She knew she could never let him go.

CHAPTER TWENTY-TWO

"You look like you finally got some sleep." Ethan said as Logan came into work early the next morning.

"Yeah, I got a little."

Ethan suspected there was more to it than a good night's sleep, but he wasn't going to press Logan too hard.

"Did Kay mention to you she hired Blake yesterday?"

"Yeah, she mentioned it last night."

"That was really nice of her."

"Logan, she didn't do it to be nice. You know Kay better than that, Blake is a talented architect and has excellent credentials."

"Even so, Blake is over the moon. She is so excited."

"Good." Ethan let the subject drop. He hadn't been as excited as Logan. It worried him that their significant others working together could cause a potential strain on their relationship. Kay had reassured him it wouldn't, but he would have to wait and see.

Simon met Blake outside her classroom door. She had planned to grab a bite to eat between classes.

"Hi,"

Blake looked up surprised, "Hi, Simon."

"Only a week left, and the semester will be over, I'm going to miss you."

"Oh thanks, I'll miss you too. I've made some great friends here."

She walked towards the exit.

"You find another job yet?"

"Yeah, I've been hired by a company to be their in-house architect."

"That's pretty impressive, I can see how academia couldn't compete with that."

Blake grinned. "It is a fantastic job; I will have a lot of creative freedom and can set my own hours pretty much."

"Wow! Do they need an engineer?"

They both laughed.

"What about your tenure?"

"Oh yeah, that is what I came to tell you. I got it!"

"Simon, that is wonderful! I am so happy for you!"

"Thanks, listen a bunch of us are going out this weekend to celebrate, join us and we can celebrate your success, too."

Blake hesitated.

"Bring your friend, it's okay."

"Okay, let me think about it."

"Tell you what, I'll send you the details and you can decide later if you can come."

"Okay, that sounds fair."

Simon took out his cell phone and started tapping. "There you have everything now. I hope to see you there."

"Thanks, again." Blake said, stepping away towards the line for a quick dinner.

Simon gave her a half-hearted wave and walked away, staring at his phone. Blake ordered a chicken salad sandwich to go. She decided she wasn't in the mood to sit among the crowd of students and faculty. She sat in her nearly empty office and ate her sandwich and thinking about Simon. He had been so nice to her, but she never fully trusted him. She always believed any man that talked to her would want to control her. But Logan wasn't like that. He was the opposite. But, despite how she felt about Logan and couldn't imagine life without him, she couldn't imagine being married again either. It was like that would be giving in; letting someone take control of her life. It was stupid, because being married to Logan wouldn't be like it had been before. She stopped herself. Why was she even thinking about marriage Logan hadn't even hinted at such a thing? What made her think he was even into marriage and a lifetime commitment. She needed to stop thinking it was all about her feelings. Suddenly, she felt like a fool and lost her appetite. She wrapped up the rest of her sandwich and threw it in the garbage.

She checked the time and gathered her things to for her next class. This was the last lecture, next week was exams and then she would be done. The school had been a place of refuge for a time. She would be grateful for that, but she was eager to get on with her life. She was ready to move on.

Her phone buzzed with a text from Logan.

"Going to be tied up for the day two days with a case. Are you free Sunday?"

She replied, "Yes, what time?"

"All day."

She smiled to herself, Logan was up to something. "Yes, I'm available all day."

***

Blake woke Sunday morning giddy with anticipation. Logan had been very secretive about his plans for them for the day and she found she was excited at the thought of a surprise. She got up showered and dressed. The one hint Logan had given her was that she should dress comfortably. We went to the kitchen to make coffee and there was a knock at the door, thinking it must be Logan she rushed to open it. Instead, there was a vase of fourteen red roses and a heart shaped balloon.

She looked out the door to see who had delivered it, but they were gone. She closed the door and took the flowers to the kitchen and fished out the card.

"Good Morning. Enjoy your coffee, but don't be late. Your chariot will await. See you soon."

She giggled and held the card to her chest. She rushed to the window to look down at the parking lot but no sign of Logan. She was too nervous to eat, and she barely touched her coffee. She decided that maybe she should add a little make-up and maybe some earrings, since she got the feeling this was not going to be a day of fishing.

An hour later there was another knock at the door.

She threw open the door, only to find it was not Logan.

"Hi, Blake. I'm Jared. I work with Logan, remember me?"

"Oh, hi. Yes, of course I remember you." She said trying to hide her disappointment.

"Logan requests that you come with me," He made a sweeping bow.

"Okay, let me get my purse."

Jared waited outside the door. When they got downstairs there was a town car with tinted windows parked along the curb, Jared opened the door for her, and she slid into the backseat covered in pink rose petals. A card was taped to the back of the front passenger seat.

"The fair ladies in waiting eagerly await your arrival."

Jared got behind the wheel and started the car.

"Jared do you have any idea what is going on."

"I'm not allowed to discuss what little I know about today's events."

"Why not?"

"It is a surprise and Logan will absolutely kill me if I tell you and I'm not about to risk being decked by Logan again."

"Logan hit you?"

"Yes, it was some time ago and I totally deserved it. He had every right to punch me."

"Do I want to know more?"

"Probably not."

"No, probably not."

She sat back and admired the rose petals; whatever Logan had planned he had certainly put a lot of effort into it. He pulled up in front of an old Victorian home that had been converted to a day spa. Standing out front waiting for her as Jared opened the door to the town car, was Stephanie, Kay, Kay's assistance Sherry and Wendy. All smiling and waving to her.

"What is going on?" She looked at Jared.

"All I know was I was asked to bring you here safely. Enjoy."

Blake walked up the sidewalk to the large porch, Kay was grinning at her.

"Welcome to a girl's day out." Kay said.

"Happy March 14th, the others cheered."

"March 14th, why is that significant?" She looked at each of their faces.

Wendy put an arm around her and guided her inside. "I don't know you'll have to ask Logan."

"And where is he?"

"You'll see him later." Kay reassured her, "for now we are going to pamper ourselves and have a wonderfully healthy lunch."

Blake couldn't help but get caught up in the spirit of the moment. They followed the spa consultant to the changing rooms, and then they all had a massage, followed by a few minutes in the steam room, then lunch by the indoor pool. They it was off for a mani/pedi and to have their hair styled.

Blake was admiring her hair in the mirror. "I don't know what Logan is up to, but I like it whatever it is."

"Speaking of Logan, you'd better come with me." Kay stood up for Blake to follow her to the changing rooms.

"I picked this out for you, I hope you like it." Kay handed Blake a garment bag.

"What is it?"

"The dress you'll need for your evening with Logan."

"What?"

"You'll see." Kay gave her a devilish grin and then left her to change.

Blake closed the door and unzipped the bag. A gorgeous, red satin dress with black sequins on the shoulder and a pair of black strappy heels to match peaked out at her.

She slid the dress on and admired herself in the mirror. She had to admit, she liked what she saw.

She fished out the shoes and found a sequined clutch as well. The butterflies in her stomach started to flutter.

The women were waiting for her when she emerged. They all fussed and complimented her on the dress.

"Kay picked it out." She insisted.

Wendy held her at arm's length, "Kay might have picked it out, but honey you fill it out." They all laughed.

"I hope Logan likes it." She was suddenly nervous that he might not.

"Are you kidding? Logan isn't going to be able to keep his hands off you!" Stephanie squeezed her hand.

"You look beautiful." Sherry added.

"Thank you all so much for spending the day with me. I don't know how Logan got you all to do this,"

"All he had to do was ask. We were happy to help make this day special for you." Kay took on a serious tone, "and we'll have to do it again, without Logan's involvement."

They all nodded and agreed to make it a regular get together for themselves.

"Now, you don't want to keep him waiting, you better get going." Wendy started shooing her towards the door."

"what about my other clothes?"

"Don't worry, we'll get them, not go your man is waiting." Wendy fussed.

Once again Jared was waiting for her and this time he was wearing a tuxedo.

"I really wish someone would tell me what is going on."

He just shook his head and closed the door behind her. He got in and turned-on soft music and drove to the upper part of town, close to Kay's office. He pulled up to a hotel and the valet stepped up and opened the door for her. Jared pulled away without a word.

A man in a dark suit and tie approved her, "Ms. Morgan?"

"Yes, please follow me."

She followed him onto the elevator.

"Where are we going?"

"I am escorting you to the Arboretum Terrace."

She nodded as if she understood what that meant.

They reached the top floor of the hotel and stepped off the elevator into a lush green restaurant. The glass ceiling and three glass walls provided a breathtaking view of the city. A three-piece band played softly in the far corner and several tables were occupied with couples enjoying the sunset.

She spotted Logan instantly, he was so handsome in his tuxedo it make her heart want to burst from her chest. His hair was slicked back, and she marveled that they made a tuxedo to fit his broad shoulders. The man in the suit faded away as Logan approached her. She found she was trembling as he smiled down at her and grasped her hands.

"You are so beautiful."

"Thank you," her voice barely a whisper.

"Shall we?" He indicated the table next to the window. She followed him and sat down as he held the chair for her.

"Logan, this is all just so...," She was at a loss for words.

He smiled, "It's not enough."

"Enough? What do you mean?"

"You deserve so much more."

"It is all so perfect." She didn't want to spoil the mood by asking too many questions.

A server appeared and offered Logan a bottle of wine. Logan nodded and the server poured some in a glass. Logan tasted it and nodded. Then poured a glass for each of them and left the bottle.

"This is so beautiful she looked out at the view." She couldn't imagine how much this place cost much less, the flowers and the day at the spa.

Logan raised his wine glass, and she did the same. "Happy March fourteenth."

"Happy March fourteenth," She said and sipped her wine. "The girls mentioned today being special because it was March fourteenth, but I don't think I understand what that means."

Logan grinned, "This is what I had wanted to do for you for Valentine's Day before things," He paused not wanting to bring the ugliness of his having shot her ex-husband to death in front of her to this special night, "This is sort of a do-over Valentines Day."

"Oh Logan, that is the sweetest thing," her words got caught in her throat and she tried to hold back a tear of joy.

Another server appeared to take their dinner order.

Logan took the liberty of ordering for them both.

"I hope you enjoyed the day with the ladies."

"I can't believe you got everyone in on this and I had no idea. Even Jared to drive the car?"

"I am capable of a few surprises."

"I would say so. The only person I haven't seen today is Ethan, should I be worried?"

"No, you won't see Ethan, he is the man by the scenes pulling all the strings, making sure everyone else was in there places today and making sure I didn't mess anything up."

"You have some amazing friends."

"We both have amazing friends." Logan corrected her.

Their meal arrived, Blake enjoyed the food but was enchanted by the atmosphere and the view. The night seemed perfect. And yet she felt a sliver of apprehension that she couldn't explain. A small piece of her past life still haunting her.

A server came to remove their plates. And Logan reached across the table and took her hand, "Shall we dance?"

"What are you serious?" She looked around the room, there was in fact a small dance floor near the band.

"Yes, I'm serious. You don't want the band the bad do you, up their play all night and no one dancing? I think it is the least we could do."

She giggled and agreed.

The band saw them approaching and started slowing the tempo of their music. Blake wondered just how perfect Logan was, he cooked, he danced. He planned wonderful days to pamper her. It was like a fairytale.

Logan saw the server's hovering, so he bent down and whispered in her ear, "do you want dessert here or at home?"

Blake followed him to the living room and sat on the sofa and, noticed he had put sweatpants and a sweatshirt on over his t-shirt and running shorts. She sighed, such a shame, he had great legs. The t-shirt did little to hide his muscular chest. She finished her tea and started getting a little drowsy.

"Hey, did you put something in my tea?"

"No! Do you think I would drug you?"

"No, sorry. What kind of tea was it?"

"Chamomile." He grinned. "Just relax and take a nap." He pulled the blanket off the back of the sofa and put it over her. Her mind wanted to protest, but her body was sinking into the sofa under the blanket.

Logan pulled out his cell phone.

"Ethan, any chance you can manage without me today?"

"Yeah, sure. Logan is everything alright?"

"Yeah, just fine. Just had something personal come up is all."

"Okay, call me if you need something."

"You got it." Logan clicked off. He grabbed a book and sat down in a chair across from the sofa. When he was sure Blake was asleep. He picked her up and carried her to his bed and returned to the living room.

CHAPTER TWENTY-THREE

Blake woke up and looked around the room was dark, but it wasn't her room. She was on the wrong side of the bed for starters, and when she reached out for the lamp; it wasn't there. She sat still for a moment and let her eyes adjust. And then she remembered. Logan. She stood up and felt her way across the room to the door. She walked down the hallway towards a room with a light. "Hello?"

A moment later Logan was standing in front of her. "Hey there, feel better?"

"Yeah, what time is it?"

"Nearly seven o'clock."

"At night?" Blake exclaimed, not believing she had slept nearly twelve hours.

"Yeah, you must have been exhausted." Logan smiled down at her. "Are you hungry?"

"I," she paused still trying to grasp that she had slept all day. "I guess so."

"Good, I've been keeping dinner warm for you."

"Really?"

"Yeah, I hope you like pork chops."

"Uh, yeah, I do."

"Good, this is my very own recipe for pork chops and gravy."

Blake was a little surprised she didn't expect Logan to cook anything that wasn't on the grill. She sat down at the kitchen table as Logan held the chair for her. The table was set with nice china plates and fresh flowers in the center.

"Um, wow. I'm impressed." She said as she watched him serve them both.

"Why, did you think all I can manage to cook is steaks on the grill and crabs in a pot?"

"Well," Blake had to admit it. "Yeah."

Logan laughed. "Fair enough."

The aroma of the food made her stomach growl, so she picked up the knife and fork and cut into the pork chop. It was tender and heavenly. "This is wonderful," she said between bites.

"I'm glad you like it." Logan smiled and lifted his wineglass. "You want to tell me why you were sitting in the cold on the beach?"

Blake anticipated the question was coming, and she was prepared to answer it.

"I wanted to clear my head a little. There have been a lot of changes in my life lately, and I really haven't faced them head on. I thought I'd take some time and do a little self-introspection."

Logan nodded; he wasn't one to argue with someone having to deal with their inner demons.

"I guess I lost track of time. The sound of the waves is very addictive."

"Yes, they are."

She waited for him to say more; she was expecting a lecture. When one didn't come immediately, she returned to her meal. Logan was concentrating too hard on his plate, but she wasn't about to push him. They finished dinner, and she helped him clean up the kitchen.

"Would you like to sit in the living room and chat?" Logan asked.

"Sure,"

They settled on the sofa; Logan turned to face her. She could tell he had something on his mind. She did too.

"Blake, I need to tell you something and as crazy as it might sound. I would like for you to hear me out."

She reached over and took his hand and nodded.

Logan squeezed her hand and continued, "I realize things have been a little interesting between us, and I can't undo the things I have done. I wish to hell I could. But I want you to know that even if it doesn't seem like it, but everything I've done; I did because I care about you." He paused and looked away for a moment, collecting his thoughts and calming his breathing.

Blake squeezed his hand but waited for him to finish.

"I'm really not good at this sort of thing. Expressing myself in words is not my strong suit." He chuckled.

"You're doing fine."

He looked at her. He could get lost in her eyes for hours. "I don't just care deeply about you, I'm in love with you and I've never been in love with someone before, so I'm probably not very good at it. But I have never felt this way about anyone in my life and I don't expect I will again regardless of how you feel about me. I didn't tell you before, because you've not had a pleasant experience in the past. But, today, when I couldn't find you and then I saw you out there near frozen, my heart stopped beating. I don't want to crowd you, but Blake, I literally cannot stand being away from you or not being able to reach out and text or talk to you. It kills me inside. I've struggled with telling you this because I didn't know how you felt. After today, I needed to tell you."

Blake watched while Logan battled his emotions while he spoke. Her heart swelled and broke for him all at the same time. Logan looked at her and lifted one corner of his very kissable mouth in a smile. His eyes pleading for her to understand.

She was still holding his hand, and she moved a little closer to him on the sofa. She smiled sweetly and caressed his cheek.

"Logan, I had a lot to think about out there on the beach. My life has changed completely, since moving here. I used to be independent minded but never in my actions. I let Jerry be responsible for everything, including me. And I was miserable. But it wasn't until he hit me, I realized what I was doing. I was allowing myself to be treated that way, and when I left him, I vowed to allow no one to have control over me like that again."

Logan's heart sank. He had a terrible feeling that she was leading up to telling him she didn't want to be in a relationship; or at least not with, him. But he held his tongue and let her continue.

"And I think I have done that since moving here. I was a little slow to start, I finally know who I am. The real me that has been hiding all these years. And it's so liberating, and wonderful and magical, and so many other things, I can't explain. A big part of that is because of you."

Logan looked at her, his brow knitting together in an unspoken question.

Blake held his hand in both of hers. "You've shown me how a real man cares for a woman. How you can love someone and not have to control them, how two people can care about each other and still be their own person. And this sounds crazy by normal people's standards, considering I am recently divorced, and my ex-husband recently died. Most people would think, the last thing I would ever want is to be involved in another relationship, especially so soon after," she took a deep breath, "everything that has happened. But I am so in love with you it's ridiculous."

Logan looked at her, "What?" He thought he had heard her wrong.

Blake raised up on her knees and let go of his hand to brace herself on his shoulders and kissed him.

Logan returned her kiss, but then pulled away.

"Wait a minute,"

"What?" Blake looked bewildered.

"What are you saying?"

"I'm saying I love you, you big lug."

"But what about that guy, Simon?"

"What?" Blake laughed. "Simon is just a friend."

"Does he know that?"

"I don't really care."

Logan grinned, "You love me, too?"

"Since the first time I met you."

"But...,"

"Stop talking," Blake said, brushing her lips against his.

Logan kissed her deeply and pulled her close so that she was resting on his chest. He liked the way she felt in his arms, on his body. The way she tasted. How she moved when he moved. It was like they were completely in sync with one another.

"Blake Morgan, I want to make love to you."

Blake sucked in her breath, excitement racing through her body.

She nuzzled his ear and kissed his neck. "If you don't soon, I might explode."

Logan lifted her and stood up, carrying her to the bedroom. He knew exactly how she felt. And he intended to satisfy them both tonight.

The End

Don't miss out!

Visit the website below and you can sign up to receive emails whenever Lynn Story publishes a new book. There's no charge and no obligation.

https://books2read.com/r/B-A-ULCK-FNDQB

BOOKS 2 READ

Connecting independent readers to independent writers.

About the Author

Lynn is a native of the Hampton Roads region of Virginia, the area which is the inspiration for the Gates Point series. She enjoys time in, on and around the Chesapeake Bay and its tributaries. When she isn't out exploring, she enjoys spending time at home with her husband in the garden.

Read more at www.stitchesandstories.com.